# *The*

MW01061123

# *and*
# *Black Comedy*

## TWO ONE-ACT PLAYS

*by Peter Shaffer*

S A M U E L   F R E N C H ,   I N C .
45 WEST 25TH STREET                    NEW YORK 10010
7623 SUNSET BOULEVARD          HOLLYWOOD 90046
*LONDON*                                               *TORONTO*

## NOTE

THE WHITE LIARS is a new play. It is loosely based on my play "WHITE LIES" (originally done in New York as a companion piece to BLACK COMEDY)—but it has been completely re-conceived and re-written. It was produced in London at the Lyric Theatre, on the 21st February 1968, in tandem with a new production of BLACK COMEDY.

I regard this new play, THE WHITE LIARS, as the final version of this material, and would like it to be played before BLACK COMEDY wherever a second play is required. The two plays represent a complete evening's entertainment, on the theme of tricks.

PETER SHAFFER

## CHARACTERS

SOPHIE: BARONESS LEMBERG

FRANK

TOM

## PLACE

The play happens in the Fortune Teller's parlour of Sophie, Baroness Lemberg, on the pier at Grinmouth, a run-down seaside resort on the south coast of England.

## TIME

The present. Around six o'clock in the evening: late September.

## NOTE ON THE "TAPE"

The tape represents whatever is happening inside Sophie's head at the moment it is heard; either present thought, or recollection. In production it is better to use a live Vassi wherever possible with an offstage mike. This makes for greater liveliness of response. The only bits on tape should really be those involving Sophie—her interjections, and her duologue at the end, beginning, "start a shop together."

# THE WHITE LIARS

# The White Liars

SCENE: *Sophie's parlour is set between two levels of the pier. It is reached from above by an iron staircase, and it is set on iron stanchions rising out of the sea. As we look at it, it seems suspended against the wet, six o'clock sky: a cluttered nest in a tangle of Victorian ironwork. The room is actually divided by a curtain into two: a little ante-room, with a bench for waiting; and the consulting room, replete with covered table on a rotting strip of carpet, and a couple of broken down chairs. Her window, streaked with salt and bird droppings, proclaims in reverse gilt letters: "BARONESS LEMBERG. PALMISTE. CLAIRVOYANTE." And in smaller letters: "LEMBERG NEVER LIES." The place is dirty and claustrophobic, deriving its mystery from the fantasy of its location, hung over the water and wrapped in sky.*

AT RISE: *As the LIGHTS come up through the cobweb of rusting iron, we see* SOPHIE *seated at her table playing patience. She is a woman of forty-seven: once beautiful, and still handsome, dressed in the blouse and skirt of a professional working woman. When she speaks, her voice is marked by a strong, but never incomprehensible, German accent. The SEAGULLS cry.*

SOPHIE. Nine on eight . . . seven on six. Good . . . Queen on Jack. So. (*She looks up expectantly. A client? Only seagulls.*) Ace on the King. Now please . . . two . . . two . . .

(*She contemplates the cards. The voice of* VASSI *steals softly into the room.*)

7

VASSI. (*TAPE.*) I like. I will like. I may like. I have lik-ed.

SOPHIE. (*Correcting him.*) Liked.

VASSI. (*TAPE.*) Liked, liked . . .

SOPHIE. Eight on seven, good. Now bloody two . . .

VASSI. (*TAPE.*) I go. I may go. I will go. I am going. Go-ing.

SOPHIE. Four on three . . .

VASSI. (*TAPE.*) I am going. I have (*Pronouncing it to rhyme with "lone."*) gone.

SOPHIE. Gone.

VASSI. (*TAPE.*) Gone. This is impossible language!

SOPHIE. (*Playing.*) Persevere, my darling. Practice is making perfect. That is an English expression. You must remember expressions: they make the language natural. But nothing vulgar, please. No idioms from the street. There is a fashion nowadays for gentlemen to use words out of the gutter—but that's not for you. I will tell you what to say, and what is a bit, as they say in England, "off."

VASSI. (*TAPE.*) I speak. I will speak. I have *spoken.* What strange word. "Spoken." Spoken . . . Spoken—I have spok—

(*She drops the cards and puts her hands to ears. Immediately the SOUND cuts off.*)

SOPHIE. (*Sharply.*) Look, you promised to stop this. You absolutely promised! . . . (*She rises and moves to the window.*) Ja—but then who am I supposed to talk to? There hasn't been one client here in four days. Not one human being. Look at it. Not one single holiday maker from this pier to the next. Nothing anywhere but water—old brown sea—like they have poured out ten million cups of tea. No wonder they call it the English Channel! Grinmouth-on-Sea, Fairyland of the south coast! Grinmouth-on-*Tea!* You hear that, Vassi? I made a joke, ja? . . . All right, don't laugh. We Germans have no sense of humour, it's well known. Only you Greeks are witty. Ja, ja.

VASSI. (*TAPE.*) Sophie, I am trying to study!

SOPHIE. I'm sorry, I'm sorry! God knows you certainly need it! I thought I'd die yesterday in front of Mrs. Steiner what you said to me. Do you know what you said? "Tell me, Sophie, who was Queen Arthur?" Unbelievable! . . . You know, my dear, if you are going to keep company with a baroness, you'd better learn how. Also, you wear too much oil on your hair. Oil's common. You're not a grocer.

VASSI. (*TAPE.*) My father's a grocer.

SOPHIE. Then your father can wear the oil. Beloved God, can we spend one day without hearing of this boring father, and his dear little food shop in Athens? Look, liebchen, no doubt you are fond of him. And that's good, because loyalty is a gentleman's character. But it is perfectly obvious he is not really your father. You don't get bones like that from a grocer. Now please don't argue, Vassi. If there is one thing I know about, it's bones. Must I remind you that my name, Lemberg, was already great in Austria under Maria Theresa. All you had in your so civilised Greece at that time, my dear, were goats. Human goats living on curd milk. All right? . . .

VASSI. (*TAPE. Teasingly.*) I go. I may go. I may go. I . . . will go.

SOPHIE. All right. Go— Go to Irina. You've been meeting her again, haven't you?

VASSI. (*TAPE.*) Yes.

SOPHIE. Any special reason?

VASSI. (*TAPE.*) No.

SOPHIE. Then why?

VASSI. (*TAPE.*) She does not know anybody in London. Look, I told you.

SOPHIE. I know, I know. She's the daughter of your father's oldest friend. Obligation. Very Greek. I'm sure.

VASSI. (*TAPE. Laughing.*) I think you're jealous.

SOPHIE. Very amusing. Please continue with your studies.

VASSI. (*TAPE. Delighted.*) I am jealous. I may be jealous. I will be jealous. I have been jealous—

(*She again blocks out the NOISE by putting her hands to her ears.*)

SOPHIE. Oh, God, God, God! Why can't I stop this? Mad woman! Talking day after day to someone you haven't even seen in five years! (*She goes to the mirror.*) Once and for all, it's over! Over, over, over, OVER!

(*A pause.*)

VASSI. (*TAPE. Stealing into her thoughts softly.*) Excuse me.

SOPHIE. Go away.

VASSI. (*TAPE.*) My name is Vassi.

SOPHIE. Enough now. Bloody *enough!*

VASSI. (*TAPE.*) I have taken the room opposite you. I am wondering, could I please watch your television set ten minutes? There is rock and roll entertainment.

SOPHIE. (*Remembering, smiling as she turns.*) Of course. Come in . . .

VASSI. (*TAPE.*) Thank you very much.

SOPHIE. (*Recalling to herself.*) Black eyes. Hair—holy cap of hair. Well-born, I don't care what he says.

VASSI. (*TAPE: Exasperated.*) Sophie, my father just sells food in a shop!

SOPHIE. Then you must be illegitimate.

VASSI. (*TAPE.*) Thank you.

SOPHIE. It's obvious. Why do you fight me, darling? Why do you resist all the time my training? I only give it for your good. Can't you understand, I know what I'm talking about! It takes one aristocrat to recognise another.

VASSI. (*TAPE.*) Does it? Well . . . I was talking to Mrs. Steiner last night. She told me certain things.

SOPHIE. Things?

VASSI. (*TAPE.*) About you.

SOPHIE. And you believed them, naturally.

VASSI. (*TAPE.*) Yes. I believed them.

SOPHIE. Naturally. A woman like Steiner, famous for lying—naturally you believed her.

VASSI. (*TAPE.*) I'll tell you what she said—

SOPHIE. I don't want to hear.

VASSI. (*TAPE.*) She said it wasn't true.

SOPHIE. I said I don't wish to listen. Lies and vulgarity. All the world is full of them!

VASSI. (*TAPE.*) She said none of it was true!— (SOPHIE *starts singing loudly.*) She said that you——that you— (*She claps her hands to ears, instantly cutting the SOUND. Silence. TAPE. Angry.*) Liar! Lying dreadful woman! . . . For months I believed you, when you shouted at me to be a gentleman like you were a lady. *Like! you! were!* . . .

SOPHIE. (*Anxiously.*) Where are you going? . . . Are you leaving?

VASSI. (*TAPE.*) Do you think I stay here with you—with a liar?

SOPHIE. (*Tearfully.*) All right. Go! But when you look back on this moment—just ask yourself this. Is it really such a crime to want to make yourself seem a little important? To try to shield yourself just a little from the sordidness of everyday life? Is it? (*With sudden briskness, snapping back into reality.*) Beloved God, look! Two whole clients! (*She looks up.* FRANK *and* TOM *come into view, above. They lounge down the stairs and stand outside her window, apparently debating whether to come in. She watches them hungrily.*) Two pounds if they take the cards. *Four,* if they take the crystal ball! Beloved God, make them come in! I promise—I swear to you— no talk one whole day, not a word, I promise it, if they come in—Vassi's my witness! (*The* TWO BOYS *start to walk away.*) *Two* days silence! *Two* whole days! . . . Come in, oh, *please!*

(*They turn back and come in.*)

Tom. Anyone home?

Sophie. One moment, please! (*She scurries about during the following, adjusting her hair, laying out the cards and the crystal ball, and finally donning her shawl.*)

(*Of the two boys,* Frank *is middle-class, soft spoken and gentle; his manner is shy, warm and immediately likeable—in great contrast to his companion, who seems casual almost to the point of brutality.* Tom *is dressed like a parakeet in brilliant colours, wears his hair very long and speaks in a heavy Midlands accent.*)

Tom. I'll go first.

Frank. Why?

Tom. Well, I've got to be back, haven't I? I mean, it can't stay the way it was this afternoon, can it? Bloody amateur time, that was.

Frank. I thought it was fine.

Tom. Did you?

Frank. More than fine. Yes.

Tom. Well, it's good I don't leave the choice up to you, then, isn't it?

Frank. That's not fair! . . . Just because I thought . . .

Tom. What?

Frank. Thought it went very well. For a rehearsal. You just suspect every compliment.

Sophie. (*Calling.*) Come in, please! (Frank *goes in.* Tom *follows him quickly.*) Good evening . . . One of you at a time, please.

Tom. (*To* Frank.) Right. I'll see you, then.

Frank. Well . . . Why don't we toss for it?

Tom. Toss?

Frank. Well, that's fair, isn't it? (Tom *shrugs sullenly.* Frank *pulls a coin from his pocket: with a nervous laugh, to* Sophie.) We're both so anxious to see you, it's a bit of a fight . . . Heads or tails?

Tom. Heads.

(FRANK *tosses*.)

FRANK. Tails! I win! (*Showing it to* SOPHIE.) True?
(SOPHIE *nods in acquiescence. To* TOM.) Look, why don't
you go for a ride on the dodgems? They'll be glad of the
custom.

(TOM *shrugs*.)

SOPHIE. Come back in ten minutes, please. Expert
divination does not take very long.
FRANK. You don't mind, do you?
TOM. You won, didn't you?

(*He lounges out.* FRANK *looks after him*.)

SOPHIE. Come along, then.
FRANK. It's an awful day, isn't it? There wasn't a soul
on the prom.
SOPHIE. (*TAPE*.) Interesting face.

(SOPHIE *seats herself at the table.* FRANK *watches* TOM
     *disappear along the lower level*.)

FRANK. Just us and the seagulls, all sitting in those
little shelters that are meant for people. They looked like
rows of old convalescents huddled down in their coat
collars.
SOPHIE. Sit down, please. (*TAPE*.) Actor maybe.
Entertainer. Something. Which?
FRANK. (*Staring out of the window*.) It's strange, from
here. How does it feel to live with the sea all round you?
There's a quotation: woe unto him who builds his house
on sand. Something like that. (*Sensing he is being rude*.)
I'm sorry.
SOPHIE. That wasn't tails.

FRANK. What?

SOPHIE. It wasn't tails. It was heads.

FRANK. (*Grins nervously.*) I know . . . I'm sorry. But I *had* to see you first. It's important.

SOPHIE. Ja?

FRANK. (*Very ill at ease.*) When we drove into town this morning, I saw your sign. It says "Advice and Consultation." It sort of gave me the idea. Well, it gave me hope, actually . . .

SOPHIE. Ja?

FRANK. I don't know . . . (*Pause.*) It seemed like a good idea when I thought of it. Now, not—not so much . . . The thing is, you mustn't be angry. I mean at what I'm going to ask.

SOPHIE. Angry?

FRANK. (*In a rush.*) I mean, I've got a suggestion—a sort of . . . Look, Baroness. I don't actually want my fortune told. I've come about something else, and you've every right to throw me out and be very annoyed, only I hope you won't be.

SOPHIE. Young mister: I have no idea what you are saying. Am I supposed to be clairvoyant or something? . . . That's my joke. I often make it.

FRANK. Oh. Yes . . .

SOPHIE. Come, come. Sit. (FRANK *sits.*) You look pale. Are you worried?

FRANK. I suppose so.

SOPHIE. Is it your professional life?

FRANK. No. Look, I'll pay you, just like it was a regular session. Actually, I thought I'd offer you a little more. Unless you'd be insulted.

SOPHIE. Why should I be insulted? Advice is as hard as divination. It is your love life? Trouble with a girl? (FRANK *shrugs.*) And your friend is involved also?

FRANK. A bit cliché, isn't it?

SOPHIE. It's not exactly unfamiliar, I admit. Two friends in love with the same girl.

FRANK. Except he's *not* in love with her. And she just

*thinks* she's in love with him. She just thinks it! . . .
She's very easily impressed. Mind you, I sort of see: he
is impressive. Like no one she's ever met before, I suppose. Bright—tough—completely natural. That's it, really,
you see: he's natural about everything. The way you can
only really be, I suppose, if you're genuine working class.
(*He smiles.*) The trouble with me is, I see everyone's
point of view. Here I am defending him already!

SOPHIE. This boy is an entertainer?

FRANK. He is a singer. Thanks to me. I mean, there's
no point being modest about it. I found him singing in an
East End pub, flat broke. A natural musician. Really
marvellous. I made a whole group for him. That's my
racket, really, you see: I'm a manager. I created The
Liars specially for him.

SOPHIE. The Liars?

FRANK. The White Liars. Four instrumentalists and
Tom. I even did the uniform. White satin—it's wild!
They're singing here tonight. Perhaps you'd like to come.

SOPHIE. Thank you: no! As far as I am concerned, the
birth of electricity meant the death of music. I had a
friend once who liked all that. He would have come and
howled his little head off for you . . . Your girl friend
helps you?

FRANK. Sue? I don't know what we'd do without her.
She drives the van, does the accounts, nursemaids the
boys—everything. She's one of those people who are
permanently turned on, you know.

SOPHIE. Turned on? You mean, like a light?

FRANK. I'll be honest. I've lived with her for two years,
and it's been the best time I've ever known.

SOPHIE. But now it is—*ending,* ja?

FRANK. Not if I can help it.

SOPHIE. Because of him?

FRANK. Look, when I first met Tom, he'd only been
down from the Midlands three weeks. He was living in a
filthy little cellar in the slums. He was absolutely miserable.

SOPHIE. So—you took him into your house?

FRANK. The stupidest thing I ever did. I gave him a room in my flat, free. The thing about Tom is he's a monster. I mean that in the Greek way. Like one of those things in a fable. He *lives* on worship! It's his food. I mean it quite literally: he can hardly get through a day without two tablespoons of sticky golden worship poured down his throat, preferably by a girl. Poor Sue walked right into it, you see. I mean, because that's a bit her scene, spooning it out. And the awful thing is, I know what's going to happen. Tom's the kind of boy—as soon as she says O.K.—as soon as she crosses that landing from our room to his—he won't be interested any more. And she's going to, Baroness. (*A pause.*) She's going to cross, any minute.

SOPHIE. So prevent it! Tell him to go!

FRANK. I can't . . . I'm just . . . incapable . . . Isn't that silly? For one thing, it's so corny: Keep Your Hands Off My Girl! I just can't! . . . And anyway, scenes like that can never do any good—what good can it do, losing your cool? You just look ridiculous . . . (*He gets up and starts pacing about.*) The thing is, he's so bloody . . . disarming. I'm like that. I get disarmed. Made just . . . incapable. You won't believe it: I lie in bed beside her at night, rehearsing scenes I'm going to have with him at breakfast. I make up whole speeches, brilliant cutting sentences—or maybe ones more in sorrow than in anger, you know—rather noble! And then in the daylight, I look at him swabbing crusts round the egg yolk on his plate, and I just can't bring them out. I mean people aren't inside your head. You know? . . . (*Pause.*) The thing is: I can't take any more. He's got to get out! He's just got to! *I've got to get him out!* (*His vehemence seems to surprise them both. He looks away from her.*) I had this wild idea. Like you—

SOPHIE. What?

FRANK. Could see it all.

SOPHIE. See?

FRANK. In the ball.

SOPHIE. (*Slowly.*) See all . . . what?

FRANK. (*Getting nervous.*) Look, the thing about Tom is—he's fantastically superstitious. I mean, ridiculous. He's always loping off to fortune tellers and palmists, every place he goes. One week it's a woman in Acton who does it with beans. The next, it's some Chinaman in Cheltenham who does it with dice.

SOPHIE. And now it's some German in Grinmouth who does it—with what exactly?

FRANK. Well, this, actually, I thought . . . (*He produces an envelope from his pocket.*) The main facts of Tom's life. It's all stuff he's told me over the past year. Provincial childhood—coalmining village—drunken dad who threw his guitar on the fire. It's pretty conventional stuff really. I thought—

SOPHIE. What? That as I'm a fake, I could not possibly find them out for myself?

FRANK. Of course not! Only using this, you'd be absolutely accurate. I mean absolutely. So exact you'd have him goggling. He's a great goggler. He'd totally believe— totally: you can't imagine it. I mean if you were to see something a bit—

SOPHIE. Ja? A bit?—

FRANK. Alarming . . . In his future.

SOPHIE. What kind of alarming, mister?

FRANK. Well, like some dangerous relationship.

SOPHIE. With a girl?

FRANK. Yes.

SOPHIE. Which, of course, he should break off immediately. If he doesn't—terrible disaster waits for him. Ja? (*Amused.*) Blood and calamity!

FRANK. It sounds ridiculous now. Like I said . . .

SOPHIE. And how much am I to receive for this absurdity?

FRANK. It doesn't matter.

SOPHIE. *How much?*

FRANK. I thought three pounds was ~

SOPHIE. Suitable?
FRANK. Five then?

(*A pause.*)

SOPHIE. Mister, I know I don't look so prosperous here in this filthy little room, but who do you think I am? Some silly gypsy bitch in a caravan, you can buy for three pounds?
FRANK. No, of couse not.
SOPHIE. (*With grandeur.*) I practise here in this hideous town, an art as old, as sacred as medicine. Look at this! This hand has the held the hand of a Royal Duchess in intimate spiritual communion. It has held Governors—Ministers of Justice—Princes of the blood! All right, I have—what is it? *"come down"* in the world! Come down to Grinmouth! Down to Pizza stalls! and grease in the air! dodge-them cars and rifle bangings and all the fun in the fairground! Every day now—if I see anybody at all!—my *noble* clients are people like old potatoes wearing paper hats. Whispering spinsters, smelling of camphor!—old red men with gin in their eyes, begging me to predict just one football pool to make them rich for life! *Rubbish people,* all of them, *killing* me to death with their middle class dreams! But one thing, mister—I may hate them, but I never cheat them. Lemberg never lies!

(*A pause.*)

FRANK. I'm sorry.
SOPHIE. That's all right. (*He goes out into the anteroom. TAPE.*) Silly cow! You've just talked yourself out of three pounds.
FRANK. (*Suddenly he returns.*) Look, it was a stupid thing to do. All right, I'm stupid. I was desperate, that's what I was. When you're that way you don't think straight. You just dream up the stupidest ideas—anything

that could work . . . (*A pause.*) I love this girl, Baroness.

SOPHIE. (*She accepts his apology.*) And this boy, what do you expect from him? Consideration? Gratitude?

FRANK. What's wrong with that? When I found him he was desperate. I set him. Formed the group for him—got him work—put money in his pocket, I gave him a home.

SOPHIE. Idiot!

FRANK. Why?

SOPHIE. (*She rises and faces him.*) Idiot, *idiot!* Look, mister, what do you want? You know in your brain in your eyes, when they're open—you know that the world is divided only into Givers and Takers, and that nothing can change it. The Givers are the world's aristocrats. I don't mean titles. You don't have to have a title to be an aristocrat. The Takers are the Peasants, emotional peasants, do you understand me? No—you don't. Because you're a Giver yourself. I can see it. It takes one to know one. And we—we, are the innocents of this earth. Over and over again its victims! What do you want? To be the first person to change a Taker into a Giver? A peasant into a prince? Idiot. They will only laugh at you, don't you know that? They say, it's your nature to give —so give! And when they have taken everything from you, then they go off. Any excuse will do. You're not a real Baroness. They can't bear to live with a liar. Anything . . . Do you see? . . .

FRANK. Yes, I suppose I do . . .

SOPHIE. (*Softly.*) No, you don't. Innocent. Never mind . . . All I say to you is this. There is only one way to deal with a Taker. Take him yourself. Show him what it is like to be used. (*She breaks off, hearing the approach of* TOM's *whistling. He comes into view, on the lower level of the pier, crawling and sliding through the struts. In his hand is a large woolly toy dog.* SOPHIE *and* FRANK *watch him through the window.*) Ja, there it is! Look at his head: Taker's head! Neat in its neatness! Taker's neck—moves quick, like a bird pecking in the seed. Those are signs, mister: head and neck. Ja, and eyes. (FRANK *stares at her, amazed.* TOM *moves on.*) I saw his eyes. So hard, the way they opened. So black.

FRANK. Grey, actually.

SOPHIE. What?

FRANK. His eyes are grey. I think.

SOPHIE. Taker's eyes. Black eyes turned all hard. I've seen it. (*Almost gaily.*) Give me the envelope. *I'll read his fortune, mister!* I'll read it for him! You come back after he's gone. (*She stretches out her hand for the envelope. He hangs back.*)

FRANK. No, I don't think so.

SOPHIE. Give! (*Suddenly reluctant, he hands it over.*) What colour is your girl?

FRANK. Blonde.

SOPHIE. More!

FRANK. She often wears a pink scarf round her head. Very fond of that. A pink scarf.

SOPHIE. Ssssh! (*They freeze as* TOM *enters the anteroom. Raising her voice.*) And you, my dear, your dominant colour is green—your lucky day of the week is Wednesday, and as I said before everything in your cards indicates activity, activity and again activity! That will be one pound, please. (*He hands her three pounds.*) It's going to be a very busy year, believe me. Lemberg never lies.

FRANK. Well, thank you, Baroness.

SOPHIE. Thank you. I wonder if your friend has returned.

FRANK. (*Raising his voice.*) Tom!

TOM. 'Allo.

SOPHIE. Ah: good. Ask him to be kind enough to wait one minute, please. (*Indicating the envelope.*) I'll call when I'm ready.

FRANK. Of course. (*He stays where he is, still reluctant.*)

SOPHIE. Goodbye.

FRANK. Yes . . . (*For* TOM's *benefit, at the curtain.*) And thank you again.

(*He goes through into the ante-room. Hastily,* SOPHIE *sits at the table, tears open the envelope and starts reading.*)

TOM. (*Sotto voce.*) Well, how is she? No good?

FRANK. (*Indifferently.*) Well they're all fakes, aren't they?

TOM. Didn't she tell you anything?

FRANK. Not much, no—

SOPHIE. (*Calling out.*) One moment, mister, please! I'll be with you immediately! (*TAPE.*) Born 1945.

TOM. Is she really hopeless?

FRANK. Impossible. She didn't get one thing right. They should really cancel her witch licence.

TOM. Hush up.

FRANK. What?

TOM. (*Sotto voce.*) She'll hear! You mustn't call them witches!

SOPHIE. (*TAPE.*) Mining village . . . Father drunkard . . .

TOM. (*Holding up the dog.*) Look what I won! There's a rifle stall at the end there, by the turnstiles. They were so glad to see me, they virtually gave it me. I'll give it to Sue.

FRANK. It looks drunk to me!

TOM. It's all that fresh air—it's knocked the poor bugger out! What's she doing in there? Is she in a trance or something?

FRANK. I don't know—I think she calls it preparing.

TOM. You mean like meditation?

FRANK. I'll bet it's just a quick zooz, poor old cow.

TOM. Shush!

SOPHIE. (*TAPE.*) Boxing Day . . . Ran away from home.

FRANK. Look, why don't you just come back with me?

TOM. Well I'm here now, aren't I? She's seen me.

FRANK. I mean it's just such a waste of money.

TOM. (*Slyly.*) There's nothing funny about her, is there? Are you sure she didn't tell you something?

FRANK. Nothing, not a damn thing!

TOM. Well you look a bit funny to me!

FRANK. I'm telling you she's just bad, that's all—plain boring! . . .

TOM. (*As the dog.*) Arf! Arf! . . . (*He "sets" the dog on* FRANK.)

FRANK. Oh, I'll be off. I can see you're hooked. I ought to have known—that will be the day when *you* pass up going to any witch, no matter how lousy!

TOM. Shush!

FRANK. All right, all right. Just don't say I didn't . . . Well, I'll see you.

(TOM *nods.* FRANK *goes.* TOM *sits lounging on the bench.*)

SOPHIE. (*TAPE.*) Pink scarf.

SOPHIE. What are you staring at, Vassi?

VASSI. (*TAPE.*) So very honest, isn't it?

SOPHIE. Honest? . . . (TOM *looks enquiringly at the noise. Lowering her voice.*) What principles! They won't prevent you spending it, will they? Terrible Sophie for making it, but sweet little Vassi that spends it! Anyway, what do you think your wonderful Oracle at Delphi was doing, one silly cow sitting in a lot of smoke saying exactly what she was paid to say? . . . And this little . . . (*Even lower.*) monster . . . Someone's got to show him, and that's going to be me! For once, my darling, a Taker gets it! You don't like that, do you? Well, too bad! It is sometimes the painful duty of the aristocracy to teach lessons! Now leave me alone.

(*She goes to the door, but is stopped by* VASSI's *voice.*)

VASSI. (*TAPE.*) I was talking to Mrs. Steiner last night and she says you are not a Baroness at all.

SOPHIE. (*Loud.*) All right! All right! (TOM *looks up startled.*) *How dare you?* (*Sotto voce.*) Good! It's understood! You can't bear to live with a fake! Just go now, right away. GO! (*Calling.*) Come in, mister! (TOM *rises and enters the parlour, leaving the toy dog on the floor in the ante-room.*) Sit down. Here is my scale of charges. (*She hands him a card.*) One pound for cards alone. Thirty shillings, cards and palms. Two pounds for crystal ball. I recommend the ball. It is more profound.

TOM. (*Agreeing.*) Yeh.

SOPHIE. (*TAPE.*) Conceited face. Cruel . . .

SOPHIE. You're an addict, I think.

TOM. Addict? You mean drugs?

SOPHIE. Divination. You go often to consult people.

TOM. (*Surprised.*) That's right, actually. Does it show?

SOPHIE. You have comparing eyes.

TOM. Oh. That's no fun, is it?

SOPHIE. (*Coldly.*) They don't disturb me, mister. When you are older, you will learn that you can't go *shopping* in the world of the occult. People with the Gift do not live in supermarkets, you know. Give me something you wear, please. A handkerchief will do.

(*Warily he hands her his handkerchief. He takes off his top coat and hangs it up.*)

SOPHIE. (*TAPE.*) Teach him. Cruel deserves cruel back.

(*He returns to the table and sits back. She takes the cover off the ball.*)

SOPHIE. There. Just a ball of glass. Except that nothing is *just* anything.

TOM. Of course not.

SOPHIE. (*Abruptly.*) Sssh! Don't speak, please . . .

(*She puts his handkerchief on the ball.*) You are a musician. (Tom *nods delightedly. Sarcastic.*) It's not such an amazing guess, mister. I've just finished reading your friend, after all. I hope he was satisfied.

Tom. Oh . . . Yeh . . .

Sophie. He has good emanations. I predict for him a very happy domestic life.

Tom. Yeh?

Sophie. Yes. (*She stares at him. A pause.*) We begin now. What month were you born?

Tom. May.

Sophie. Taurus. Impetuous. Sometimes ruthless.

Tom. Twenty-fifth.

Sophie. Gemini. Interesting. (*She removes the handkerchief and peers savagely into the ball.*) It's very disturbed. Much confusion. 1945. You were born in 1945?

Tom. (*Amazed.*) Yes!

Sophie. It's ritualistic, the ball. Often it gives first the date of birth, then the place. Ja, exactly. Now I see a house—a little narrow house in a dirty street. At the end, a huge wheel turning in the sky. A coal wheel!—a coal village . . . I see I'm not too far from the truth. (Tom *can only nod, speechless.*) There is no woman in the house. Your mother is dead, ja? Your father, still alive. At least I see a man in working clothes. A bad face. Brutal face. Thick like a drunken man. (*They exchange stares.* Tom *is very disturbed.*) And now? I see a child. A little pale face. Eyes of fear, looking here—there—for escape. Such a frightened face. He ill-treated you, this father? He beat you? (Tom *rises and begins to pace about.*) What is this now? . . . A fire. Something burning on it . . . It looks like . . . a guitar. (*He turns on her, startled.*) Can that be right, a guitar? What is that? Some symbol of your music talent?

Tom. No . . .

Sophie. I disturb you, mister.

Tom. You see that?

Sophie. Very plain.

Tom. But you can't. You just *can't* . . . Because it's here— It's in my head. It's in here!

Sophie. And for me it is *there!* Mister, you can lock nothing away. Time that happened once for you, happens *now* for me! Why did he do that, your father? To stop you being a musician? To hurt you? You are upset. Maybe I should stop now?

Tom. No, go on. What else do you see?

Sophie. You left home in the Midlands. Came to London.

Tom. Boxing Day. Lunch in Euston Station. Veal and ham pie.

Sophie. But you were fortunate in your friends. Recent time has been good for you: the ball is golden . . . But now . . . oh!

Tom. What?

Sophie. Not any more. Not gold, now. Going.

Tom. Can you see anything particular?

Sophie. Gold to grey. Dark. Now pink in dark. Pink hair—no, pink scarf—pink something, running, but into dark . . . You have a girl friend? (*He shrugs, then nods.*) She is in flight. I see her shadow, running in the dark. And after, another shadow: desire running too. It's— *You*, I think! Running! running! one shadow trying to take the other! But now—one more, ja, comes— Oh, it's so confused!

Tom. Tell me!

Sophie. Ssssh! (*Peering fiercely.*) This new shadow is much bigger. Ja: man. He grows—swarms up over you and her both—enormous red shadow up over everything! Over the grey, over the pink, over the dark, the red—the—red, the—red—*red*—RED!! (*She breaks off with a cry of distress.*)

Tom. What is it?

Sophie. (*In a tone of awe.*) I have seen it! . . . The bloodflash. I have seen it.

Tom. The blood?—

Sophie. Bloodflash. The most rare vision in divination.

Red blood, drowning the ball. I have read about this, but never have I seen it till now, running over the glass . . . It means—the most terrible warning.

TOM. Warning?

SOPHIE. (*She rises impressively.*) You are doing something that is not good, mister. If you con'inue—disaster will strike at you. Disaster. And very soon! I mean it, mister. I'm sorry. (*A pause. He lowers his head, almost as if he is in tears.*) If there is anything in your emotional life which is not what it should be—

(*But* TOM *is not crying. He is laughing violently—laughing, laughing, laughing, until he nearly chokes. She stares at him, scandalised; finally, the noise subsides.*)

TOM. How much did he pay you?

SOPHIE. Pay?!

TOM. Well, how did he set it up? He must have offered you a few quid on the side. He couldn't have expected you to do it for nothing.

SOPHIE. What do you mean, please?

TOM. (*Rising, wiping his eyes with the handkerchief.*) All the same, it's fantastic! . . . I mean, what's the point? Is it supposed to be a joke? Fun and games by the sea?

SOPHIE. Mister, are you suggesting I've been bribed?

TOM. I'm not suggesting it. I'm saying it!

SOPHIE. How dare you? How absolutely bloody dare you?

TOM. Because I absolutely bloody know, that's how! There's only one person in the world I've ever told those things about my childhood, and that's Frank.

SOPHIE. (*Loftily.*) Oh, mister, to a professional eye like mine, Truth does not have to be *told*. It is evident.

TOM. I dare say. And what if it *isn't* the truth?

(*A long pause.*)

SOPHIE. I beg your pardon?

Tom. What if it's a zonking great lie? Like every word of that story?

Sophie. I don't believe it.

Tom. It's true.

Sophie. Impossible. You say this to discredit me.

Tom. Why should I do that?

Sophie. Look, mister—what I see, I see. Lemberg never lies!

Tom. No, but *I do!*

(*A pause.*)

Sophie. You mean—your father is not a miner?

Tom. No. He's a very rich accountant living near Lichfield. (*He sits again, indolently.*)

Sophie. And your mother is not dead?

Tom. Not in the biological sense, no. She likes her game of golf, and gives bridge parties every Wednesday.

Sophie. But your accent!

Tom. (*Dropping it completely.*) I'm afraid that's as put on as everything else. I mean, there's no point changing your background if you're going to keep your accent, is there?

Sophie. Beloved God!

Tom. (*Smiling.*) Actually, it slips a bit when I'm drunk, but people just think I'm being affected.

Sophie. (*Astounded.*) You mean to say . . . you live your whole life like this? One enormous great lie from morning to night?

Tom. Yes, I suppose I do.

Sophie. *Unimaginable!*

Tom. Does it worry you?

Sophie. Doesn't it worry *you?*

Tom. Not particularly. Should it? . . . I mean I regard it as a sort of . . .

Sophie. White lie?

Tom. Yes, very good! A white lie . . .

Sophie. But why? In heaven's name, why? Why? WHY?

Tom. Well, it's a question of image really. When I was a kid, in pop music you had to be working class to get anywhere at all. Middle class was right out. Five years ago, no one believed you could sing with the authentic voice of the people if you were the son of an accountant. . . . And here we are!

Sophie. Incredible! And your poor parents, do they know that you have abolished them completely? Like they never existed?

Tom. No, but it doesn't matter. They've abolished *me*, after all. How real am I to them? Dad calls me "Minstrel Boy" whenever I go home, because he finds it embarrassing to have a singer for a son. And Mother tells her bridge club I'm in London studying music—because studying is a more respectable image for her than performing in a cellar. Both of them are talking about themselves, not me. And that's fine, because that's what everybody's doing all the time, everywhere. Do you dig? (*He gets up to go.*)

Sophie. But at least you've told your girl friend? She knows the truth?

Tom. Sue? No.

Sophie. You mean you just sit there, holding her hand, telling her lies about your terrible childhood?

Tom. She likes it. She finds it all very sad.

Sophie. That's the most disgusting thing I ever heard! Do you think you can borrow suffering—just to make yourself attractive?

Tom. I know I can. (*He reaches for his coat.*)

Sophie. He was right, your friend. You're a monster.

(*The* Boy *turns. A pause.*)

Tom. Is that what he said?

Sophie. His word exact. A monster.

Tom. (*Laughing.*) I don't believe it.

Sophie. Of course not. All the same, to me it's obvious. I can see it now quite clearly.

TOM. As clearly as you saw my past life in that ball?

SOPHIE. Don't be impertinent. Remember, please, who you are speaking to. You are in the presence of a Baroness!

TOM. *Am I?* . . . (SOPHIE *glares at him.*) I'm sorry.

SOPHIE. The session is at an end.

(*He goes into the ante-room, bewildered, shutting the door behind him.*)

SOPHIE. (*TAPE.*) Pig! Pig! Common pop-pig!

SOPHIE. (*Calling.*) There will be no charge!

TOM. (*Calling back.*) Oh, thank you! . . . (*To himself.*) Monster? . . . What a silly word!

(*On the Tape* VASSI *giggles.*)

SOPHIE. Be quiet, Vassi!

TOM. (*Working it out.*) Me and Sue . . . She had to see disaster for me and Sue . . .

(VASSI *giggles louder.*)

SOPHIE. Giggle, giggle, always giggle! Bloody Greeks, is that all you can do?

TOM. *Jealous!*—he must be! That's the only possible ex— Christ!

VASSI. (*TAPE. Laughing.*) The bloodflash! Very rare, oh, very rare the bloodflash!

SOPHIE. (*Furious.*) For Christ's sake, Vassi, will you be quiet?

TOM. (*Storming back into the parlour.*) For Christ's sake, what did he tell you?

(*The GIGGLES stop. Silence.*)

SOPHIE. Will you go now, please? Absolutely at once.

TOM. All right, just tell me this. How long's he known

about me and Sue? Did he say? A couple of weeks? A month? I mean, Jesus, to be that hidden—not to give one sign. Just wait, day after day—build up and build up, keep your face smiling— And then come down here for the day, pull a stunt like this—thinking about it all the way down in the van, I suppose . . . I mean, *who is he?*

(*The WIND stirs slightly. We hear GULLS.*)

SOPHIE. A Giver.

TOM. What?

SOPHIE. A Giver, mister. Impossible for you to imagine, of course. Someone who just gives over and over to the end. Hidden, you call him. Of course . . . Just because he is too proud to show you the pain he feels. He now is walking by the sea, asking that same question: *"Who is he? What does he want?* I give him everything. Admiration. Not enough. Security. Not enough. I take him out of a slum—absolutely broke!—give him my own flat to share, not one penny to pay in rent—not enough! I make him a job. A whole group I form for him—white satin—engagements—everything so he can fulfill his life, not just sing for shillings in a filthy pub—but of course, not enough. Never enough! Never!"

TOM. He told you that?

SOPHIE. Ja, mister; he told. The poor idiot. He doesn't know about you—people like you. Pay the rent. "More, please!" Hellas Restaurant. "More, please!" Shop at Jaeger's, twenty pounds one jacket. Riding lessons in Richmond Park, two pounds one hour! Seats for the theatre, that boring Elektra—of course we must sit close to watch the faces—seventy shillings for two places, just to see bad make-up! Excursions to Brighton, trips in taxicabs all over London to see the Christmas lights! Stupid reindeer hanging down into the fog, a middle-class nightmare, four pounds six on the meter! . . . And always more. Always the same cry of More! Take and take, and take, until the cows are at home. And then what? Surprise! "Sophie, I've met this girl Irina. She's the daughter of my father's oldest friend. We are suited to each other, absolutely. We are both young. We both tell the truth. We don't pretend to be Baronesses. And so, bye-bye! Rent a shop in Soho, start a grocer's—such a brilliant career for a young man of refinement! (*She stops in distress.* TOM *stares at her, stupefied.*) I give you this as an example. It happened to someone I know . . . That is more or less the story. More or less.

TOM. This isn't happening.

SOPHIE. And that is Givers and Takers.

TOM. This room. Like it's sinking into the sea. Nothing makes sense here.

SOPHIE. All I tell you is this, I know you. Mister Taker. You and your law: Givers must be punished. All right, so punish him, your friend! Destroy his happiness, you can't help it!

TOM. (*Quickly.*) You're bonkers!

SOPHIE. Bonkers?

TOM. Bonkers—mad!

SOPHIE. I live alone. It's well known, people go mad alone.

TOM. I'm off! (*He makes for the door in a rush, pause, unexpected, scarcely explicable.*)

SOPHIE. Ja, go! The truth is unbearable, isn't it?

TOM. The truth, the what?

SOPHIE. It's an unfamiliar word to you, I dare say.

TOM. The truth? Jesus God! How clear it all is to you, isn't it? . . . All right, only just for the record, for the record, that's all - I'll give you three straight facts, and how you twist them is your business. O.K. I met him. I wasn't broke. I wasn't living in a slum. And I'd formed my group, a good year before I ever set eyes on him.

SOPHIE. The White Liars.

TOM. That's right.

SOPHIE. White Liars, *liars* is right!

TOM. (*Protesting.*) We had a regular gig every Friday

at the Iron Duke in the Commercial Road. You can check on that if you like.

SOPHIE. Black liars! Black! Not white! . . .

TOM. (*Insistently.*) He used to come every weekend with Sue, and sit in the corner listening to us. I just remember eyes, eyes—his brown ones and her big blue ones, and they'd sit there and groove on us for hours, just like they were the only people in the world who knew about us . . . (*Softening.*) Yeh—that's it!—like we were simply part of their private world, with no existence anywhere else . . .

SOPHIE. (*TAPE.*) Eyes—hurt eyes— Like Vassi.

TOM. Then suddenly, one night, he comes over to me—says his name's Frank—he's a free lance journalist, and wants to do a whole article on The Liars for one of the Sunday Papers. What they call a Study in Depth. It'll mean living around us for a while—did I mind? Well, it sounded great to me. I said fine. And that's how it all began—with me chasing publicity! . . . A whole month —no, longer—he just followed us about, *observing*. Endless notes in a little book. Always grinning. Silly, you know, but very likeable. He was a mad talker: you couldn't stop him, for anything. I used to tell him, a journalist is supposed to listen, not yap all the time, but he'd just laugh. "I like talking," he'd say: "It's the best thing in the world, after eating." I was living out in Winchmore Hill then, with my Aunt Daisy. Too much glazed chintz, but definitely not a slum. The only kind of music she likes is the sort you can chew teacakes to. In the end I left and moved in with him. I hadn't been there a week before I discovered he owed three months' rent.

SOPHIE. No!

TOM. Which I paid.

SOPHIE. I don't believe you.

TOM. And a week after that I found out he wasn't really a journalist at all. He worked with Sue in a boutique in the Kings Road.

SOPHIE. That's not true.

TOM. 'Til he was sacked.

SOPHIE. You're making it up!

TOM. Why should I do that?

SOPHIE. (*Hostile.*) I don't believe you. I don't *believe!*

TOM. Look, can't you dig? From the moment Frank came in here this evening, he handed you a parcel of *lies*. One after another.

SOPHIE. Fibs, maybe. That's possible.

TOM. Lies.

SOPHIE. Stories.

TOM. *Lies!* Zonking great lies!

SOPHIE. (*Suddenly furious.*) All right, lies, so what? *So what?* So he tells a couple of—of tales just to make himself a little more important—just to shield himself a little from the sordidness of life! What a crime, mister! What a terrible crime!

TOM. (*Exploding.*) It's not a crime: it's a bore! You can't *live* with liars. It's impossible!

SOPHIE. Oh, ho! ho! ho!

TOM. Not really *live!*

SOPHIE. Thank you! Thank you for the lecture! You dare! *You! dare!* talk about liars. You, with your coal mines, guitar on the fire—your whole disgusting childhood!

TOM. *His!*

SOPHIE. What?

TOM. *His. His* lies. All of them.

SOPHIE. *His* lies. About *your* childhood?

TOM. (*Softer.*) His and hers together. Theirs.

SOPHIE. (*Carefully.*) Mister, I don't know what you're saying!—

(*An enormous silence. Faintly we hear the GULLS. He stares at her.*)

TOM. If I said they'd made me up, would you get it? . . . If I said—they'd made *me* make me up. That's

nearer . . . I don't know. Sometimes I see it, just for a
second, a bit of it. Then it clouds over, just like in your
ball— (*He crosses slowly to the crystal ball on the table.*)
If only that thing really worked. If it could really show
Why. The shape of Why.

SOPHIE. That's what it does, mister.

TOM. Yes, but to me . . . (*He sits and uncovers the
crystal. Slowly he picks it up.*) If I had the gift—just for
five minutes to see the whole thing—her and him and
me . . . How does it work? Colours, isn't it? Red for
rage, black for death? . . . What for fake? Brown. That's
good. Sullen brown: the phoney sound I put on when I
came South, mainly because I couldn't stand my own
voice. (*Accent.*) Butch brown! colour of the Midlands
. . . (*Dropping it.*) My grandpa used to talk like that,
much to my mother's shame: I worked it up from him. It's
what first turned them on: Frank and Sue, especially
Frank. He used to sit on the end of my bed with his pencil
and notebook, just grooving on it. Bogus journalist inter-
viewing bogus miner! "You're so lucky," he'd say: "so
lucky to be born a Prole. The working class is the last
repository of instinct." I'd just shrug in my flannel pyjamas. Shrugs are perfect. You can imply anything with a
good shrug: repository of instinct—childhood misery—
whatever's wanted. (*He sets down the ball.*) What colour's
that? The want? The crazy want in someone for an image
to turn him on? Yeh—and the crazy way you play to it,
just to make him feel good. Green, I bet you. Green for
nausea . . . (*Simply.*) I watched him make up my childhood. "Where were you born?" he'd ask me. Then right
away, he'd answer himself. "Some godawful little cottage,
I suppose: no loo, I suppose, no electric light, I suppose."— "I suppose" meaning "I want." And me, I'd
shrug. Shrug, shrug: up goes his slum. Shrug, shrug:
down comes dad's belt: ow! Anything. I made bricks out
of shrugs. Slagheaps. Flagellant fathers and blanketless
winters, and stolen crusts gnawed in the outside lav! His
eyes would pop. Hers too—Sue's: no, hers were worse.

They'd brim with tears. She was the world's champion brimmer! She cried the first night . . . She had this flat on her own, right near the boutique. One night I'd been over for spaghetti, and I'd played a bit to her after. Suddenly—chord of E major fading into the Chelsea drizzle —she's looking down at me, and her voice is all panty. "You were born with that," she says. "There's the natural music of working people in your hands." And down comes her hair—a curtain of buttermilk over my mouth. And there it is. The want. I know it right away: the same want as his, all desperate under her hair—"Give it me. An image. Give me an image. Turn me on." What do you do? Buttermilk hair in the churn of your mouth, what *do* you *do?* Mouth opens—starts to speak—aching with its lies— the ache to please. (*Accent.*) "You *understand,*" it says, dead sincere. "Christ, you understand! . . . I'll tell you. The only encouragement my dad ever gave me was to throw my guitar on the fire! It wasn't much of an instrument, of course, but it was all I could afford . . ." (*Dropping it.*) And blue! blue, blue, blue for all the tears in her sky—dropping on me! spattering me! lashing the Swedish rug like rain on a Bank Holiday beach! I was soaked. I really was. I went to bed with her to get dry. Honest. (*Slight pause. His voice betrays increasingly more desperation. The LIGHT has faded considerably.*) That was five weeks ago. When did he find out? *She* didn't tell him. She wouldn't dare . . . He guessed. Well, of course he guessed! They know each other completely. They *are* each other! . . . Yes. (*A pause. They look at each other.*) Once I'd spoken—actually spoken a lie out loud—I was theirs. They got excited, like lions after meat, sniffing about me, slavering! I suppose I could have stopped it any time. Just by using my own voice— But I didn't. Colour the ball yellow. Well . . . I didn't want to hurt them . . . But why not? . . . Who was I? I didn't exist for them. I don't now! (*He rises violently.*) They want *their* Tom: not me. Tom the idol. Tom the Turn-on. Tom the Yob God, born in a slum, standing in his long-suffering maltreated skin—all tangled hair and natural instinct—to be hung by his priests in white satin! . . . Yeh: that's the real colour for it all. *White*. Our uniform for The Liars. He designed it—she made it—I wear it. Come tonight: you'll see me in it. Knee-breeches: Beau Brummel collar; frothy white lace round the working-class throat! (*Pause*.) I know I looked good in it, but believe it or not, the first morning I put it on, they actually kneeled down in front of me! Both of them! He was clapping his hands and yelling "Fantastic! Fantastic! Fantastic!" over and over—and she was fitting me into it, her mouth full of pins. "Don't you ever tell me you were born in a miner's cottage!" he shouts at me. "You're a natural aristocrat, Tommy!" (SOPHIE *stares at him with sudden attention*.) And she—looking up, all blue eyes and spitting pins—she says: "He's right, Tom. I bet you were born on the wrong side of the blanket!"

SOPHIE. (*Soft*.) *No!*

TOM. Yes! "Except you're never going to get the coal-dust out of your skin, are you? I can see it now in your pores!"

SOPHIE. (*Shaking her head*.) No!

TOM. (*Almost yelling*.) Oh yes: she could *see* it! (*He thrusts his bare arm at her*.)

SOPHIE. I don't believe you! People just don't behave like that.

TOM. You just can't imagine it, can you? To be a prisoner of somebody else's dream.

SOPHIE. (*TAPE*.) Out . . . Out . . . Get him out!

TOM. Because that's what it's really like with your beautiful Givers. They give you your role. That's what they give. They make you up, till you're just acting in a film projected out of their eyes. I was a prisoner on Wet Dream Island! . . .

SOPHIE. Stop it, mister! . . . Words on words on words on words! What *he* did, What *she* did, What *they* did—and all just to escape the guilt of what you did.

TOM. I did?

SOPHIE. It's very simple, mister. You had a friend, he had a girl. You stole her. That's all.

TOM. (*Quietly.*) Can you really think that? After all I've told you? Can you really believe they were lovers? (*Pause.*) Oh, love, you really are in the wrong business, aren't you?

SOPHIE. I saw his pain here. Pain. In here. Pain!

TOM. *For who?* Do you think it's *her* he wants?

(*A pause. She nods, in Teutonic comprehension.*)

SOPHIE. And if he can't have you, she must not. I see. Poor idiot.

TOM. Poor mad sod.

SOPHIE. Actually he has not guessed you slept with her. He just feared you would.

TOM. And that made him pull the whole thing down. Thank God he has. I'd never have done it. I liked it all too much. (*Accent.*) Much too much. All that lovely attention! (*A pause. He drops the accent.*) "Monster" . . . That's one thing he didn't lie about. (*He gets up, shrugging; smiling faintly.*) Well. I've still got a concert. (*He puts on his coat.*) It's going to be a strange ride back in the van. The last.

SOPHIE. The last?

TOM. Obviously.

SOPHIE. Ja.

TOM. So . . . (*He looks at her scale of charges, then takes out money and puts two pounds on the table.*) Goodbye. (*He smiles at her.*)

SOPHIE. (*Absently.*) Ja, ja . . .

(*He goes, pulling his coat about him. We see him pass through the ante-room and out up the stairs. He disappears. NIGHT has fallen. Slowly SOPHIE prepares to leave too, tidying a little, and putting on her own coat, an old bitten garment of fur. Suddenly TOM's voice whispers in her ear.*)

Tom. (*TAPE.*) They make you up. They make you up. They make you up. Make you up.

Sophie. (*Whispering too.*) No.

Tom. (*TAPE.*) Make you . . .

Sophie. No, no!

Tom. (*TAPE.*) You can't imagine it, can you? To be the prisoner of someone else's dream?

Sophie. Prisoner, ja! Not him of me, but me of him, that's true. Slave to him—complete slave. I lived only for him. It's inconceivable how we accuse ourselves, we Givers!

Tom. (*TAPE.*) Your beautiful Givers. They give us our role. That's what they give.

Sophie. Not me!

Tom. (*TAPE.*) Till we're just acting in a film projected out of their eyes!

Sophie. Ja, but not me. I never did that. I deny it absolutely! I never did that with Vassi. (*She goes firmly to the door, carrying her handbag.*)

Vassi. (*TAPE.*) Oh, Sophie, please listen! I am *not* an aristocrat! My father just sells food, that's all.

Sophie. (*TAPE.*) You are!

Vassi. (*TAPE.*) How can I be?

Sophie. (*TAPE.*) You are, you are!

Sophie. (*Vehemently.*) *You were!* (*She slams the door again, standing slumped against it.*) That face of yours, so white!—that holy cap of hair. *There* are my witnesses. The wrists so delicate, the gestures always so finished— do you think they were in my head only? They were *signs*, liebchen! Signs for the real nobility, what most people never see, what I watched at four o'clocks, when you sighed in your sleep like a prince . . . I loved you.

Sophie. (*TAPE.*) You wear too much oil on your hair, oil is common.

Sophie. I loved you.

Sophie. (*TAPE.*) Can we hear no more of this boring father?

Sophie. I loved you.

SOPHIE. (*TAPE.*) You've been seeing that slouchy little Irina. I know she attracts you. The grocer's son kisses the village dumpling!

SOPHIE. *I loved you!*

SOPHIE. (*TAPE.*) My family was great under Maria Theresa. All you had in your so civilized Greece were goats—human goats!

SOPHIE. I LOVED YOU!

SOPHIE. (*TAPE.*) If you are going to keep company with a baroness, you'd better learn how!

VASSI. (*TAPE.*) But you're not! Not! *Not!*

SOPHIE. I'm not what?

VASSI. (*TAPE.*) Mrs. Steiner told me you were just a Jewish girl called Weinberg. Not Lemberg—Weinberg.

SOPHIE. And you believed her?

VASSI. (*TAPE.*) Oh, Sophie, of course. I've known it for months. Everyone knows it. Do you think I care? It's funny.

SOPHIE. Funny?

VASSI. (*TAPE.*) Of course!—the way you shouted at me to be a gentleman like you were a lady. (*Teasingly.*) How dare you? You really are a dreadful woman, you know that? . . . (*Warmly.*) But now it's finished. Now at last we can speak truth, and I can really know you. You are No-One—just like me—and that's *lovely* . . . Come here . . .

SOPHIE. Don't.

VASSI. (*TAPE.*) Sophie, come to me. Come on! Come, come, come, come, come!

SOPHIE. Don't touch me—common hands! Common grocer's hands! Put them on Irina— Ja, there they belong! (*She sits again, completely involved in recalling the scene.*) I'm no one: is that it?

VASSI. (*TAPE.*) I didn't mean that.

SOPHIE. I'll show you Miss No-One!

VASSI. (*TAPE.*) Sophie!—

SOPHIE. Go to Irina— *There's* Miss No-One—if you want Miss Absolutely No-One! Marry *her!* (*She claps*

*her hands over her mouth: but the voice goes on relent-*
*lessly recalling what she said.*)

SOPHIE. (*TAPE.*) Start a shop together in Soho! Two
little grocer people together! Perfect! Ja, and me, I'll
come every week and buy my suppers from you. One
pound of cod's roe! One pound of goat's cheese!

VASSI. (*TAPE.*) You're excited now, and ridiculous!

SOPHIE. (*TAPE.*) Thank you.

VASSI. (*TAPE.*) Calm down! Be a baroness still if you
want it so much. It doesn't matter to me! You're still *my*
Sophie!

(*A pause. She sits rigid, remembering the rest of it.*)

SOPHIE. (*TAPE. Hard.*) Do me the favour to pack
your suitcase and go.

VASSI. (*TAPE.*) You don't mean this!

SOPHIE. (*TAPE.*) Immediate.

VASSI. (*TAPE.*) Go? . . .

SOPHIE. (*TAPE.*) Right away please, now. At once!

VASSI. (*TAPE.*) Sophie!—

SOPHIE. (*TAPE.*) I mean it. Get out—I want you out.
Get out. Get out. Get out. Get out! . . . *Get out!* (*Hol-
low, fading.*) GET OUT!

SOPHIE. Your eyes— It was in your eyes! (*In amazed
discovery.*) *You* loved *me!* . . . (*Silence.*) Oh, Vassi,
come back. I didn't mean it. I was angry— I'm stupid—
you know me, my tongue goes off with me, always away.
(FRANK *appears on the lower level and walks slowly round
to the ante-room.*) I don't know what I say . . . I promise—there won't be a baroness anymore. Just Weinberg.
Awful old Weinberg, Fraulein No-One . . . (*In tears.*)
And it'll be all right, you'll see. You'll really see. Oh,
Vassi . . . *Please!* . . .

(FRANK *enters the ante-room. He sees the toy dog and for*
*a second assumes* TOM *is still inside. He listens but*
*hears nothing. Tentatively, he opens the door.*)

FRANK. Hello? (*She pays no attention.*) He went, then.

SOPHIE. (*More to herself.*) Ja. He went.

FRANK. Just now?

SOPHIE. Packed his little suitcase and went.

FRANK. Suitcase?

SOPHIE. (*TAPE.*) Saw him only once. Snack bar window.

FRANK. What happened?

SOPHIE. (*TAPE.*) Irina giving him ice cream on a long spoon.

FRANK. Well?

SOPHIE. (*TAPE.*) Laughing together.

FRANK. Baroness!

(*He snaps on the LIGHT. With difficulty she focusses on him.*)

SOPHIE. He will leave.

FRANK. Tom?

SOPHIE. Tonight.

FRANK. Tonight?

SOPHIE. Isn't that what you wanted?

FRANK. Yes, of course! . . . No! I mean—I didn't mean *that*. (*With increasing nervous distress.*) No. I may have said,—well, I *did* say— But all I wanted was, well, just for him to lay off Sue, that's all. I mean, it wasn't even that, really. It wasn't that I regarded him as a threat or anything, not as a threat to me. I'm—I'm just worried about Sue: *you* know. She's not absolutely mature yet—she's easily impressed. I don't want her to get hurt . . .

SOPHIE. (*Regarding him sadly.*) Oh, mister. Mister.

FRANK. What did he say about me? (*Pause.*) You don't want to believe everything *he* says, you know. (*Pause.*)

SOPHIE. A lonely future, mister, believe me.

FRANK. (*Hopelessly. Slowly he retreats to the door and opens it.*) He's not really going, is he?

SOPHIE. Weinberg never lies.

(FRANK *goes into the ante-room. The toy dog is waiting for him. He picks it up, and goes out with it into the night.* SOPHIE *sits alone at her table. The LIGHTS fade on Grinmouth pier.*)

*CURTAIN*

# PROPERTY LIST

*On Stage*—ANTE ROOM
  Bench—R., angled so that it is parallel to the imaginary wall
  Magazines—on bench and on the floor underneath.

*On Stage*—PARLOUR
  Round table—centre

  *On it:*
    Green beize cover
    Two packs of playing cards—one laid out for patience
    Crystal ball on wooden base
    Black velvet cover for crystal ball
    Fan
    ashtray
    Carafe of water with glass over the top
    Box of chocolates

  Paraffin stove—Downstage Right

  *On it:*
    Pot of coffee; enough coffee for two cups

  Two wicker chairs
    One large one set on the Right of centre table. Over the
    back SOPHIE's shawl. Cushion on seat.
    Small one, Upstage Left against back wall.
  Two tier set of shelves—Upstage centre against back wall.

  *Top shelf:*
    Milk jug with milk
    Sugar bowl with sugar
    Teacup, saucer and teaspoon
    Sewing things (dressing)

  *Bottom shelf:*
    Magazines, coffee jar, sugar packet, etc. Everything on
    this shelf is dressing only.

Other dressings include pictures on the wall, rug under the
table, coat hooks on back wall.

At opening of play SOPHIE's coat is set on one of the hooks—her scarf in the pocket. SOPHIE's bag is set on small wicker chair—inside: lipstick and scent.

Light switch on Left hand upright of door adjoining parlour and ante-room—on parlour side.

*Off stage* R.:
Large toy dog

## PERSONAL PROPS

SOPHIE—two cigarettes

TOM—two cigarettes, two pound notes in money clip

FRANK—envelope containing notes for SOPHIE, three pound notes in wallet

# BLACK COMEDY

# BLACK COMEDY

## CAST
### *(In Order of Appearance)*

BRINDSLEY MILLER ............. *Michael Crawford*

CAROL MELKETT ................. *Lynn Redgrave*

MISS FURNIVAL ................. *Camila Ashland*

COLONEL MELKETT .................... *Peter Bull*

HAROLD GORRINGE ............... *Donald Madden*

SCHUPPANZIGH .................... *Pierre Epstein*

CLEA ........................... *Geraldine Page*

GEORG BAMBERGER ............... *Michael Miller*

PLACE: Brindsley Miller's apartment in South Kensington, London.

TIME: Nine-thirty on a Sunday night.

46

# DESCRIPTION OF CHARACTERS

BRINDSLEY MILLER: A young sculptor (late twenties), intelligent and attractive, but nervous and uncertain of himself.

CAROL MELKETT: His fiancee. A young debutante; very pretty, very spoilt; very silly. Her sound is that unmistakable, terrifying, deb. quack.

MISS FURNIVAL: A middle-aged spinster. Prissy; and refined. Clad in the blouse and sack skirt of her gentility, her hair in a bun, her voice in a bun, she reveals only the repressed gestures of the middle-class spinster—until alcohol undoes her.

COLONEL MELKETT: Carol's commanding father: brisk, barky, yet given to sudden vocal calms which suggest a deep and alarming instability. It is not only the constant darkness which gives him his look of wide-eyed suspicion.

HAROLD GORRINGE: The camp owner of an antique-china shop, and Brindsley's neighbour, Harold comes from the North of England. His friendship is highly conditional and possessive: sooner or later, payment for it will be asked. A specialist in emotional blackmail, he can become hysterical when slighted, or (as inevitably happens) rejected. He is older than Brindsley by several years.

SCHUPPANZIGH: A middle-class German refugee, chubby, cultivated, and effervescent. He is an entirely happy man, delighted to be in England, even if this means being employed full time by the London Electricity Board.

CLEA: Brindsley's ex-mistress: late twenties; dazzling, emotional, bright and mischievous. The challenge to her to create a dramatic situation out of the darkness is ultimately irresistible.

GEORG BAMBERGER: An elderly millionaire art collector, easily identifiable as such.

## THE SET

The action of the play takes place in Brindsley's apartment in South Kensington, London. This forms the ground floor of a large house now divided into flats. Harold Gorringe lives opposite; Miss Furnival lives above.

There are four ways out of the room. A door at the Left, Upstage, leads directly across the passage to Harold's room. The door to this, with its mat laid tidily outside, can clearly be seen. A curtain, Upstage Centre, screens Brindsley's studio: when it is parted we glimpse samples of his work in metal. To the Right of this an open stair shoots steeply up to his bedroom above, reached through a door at the top. To the Left, Downstage, a trap in the floor leads down to the cellar.

It is a gay room, when we finally see it, full of colour and space and new shapes. It is littered with marvellous objects—mobiles, mannikins, toys, and dotty bric-a-brac —the happy paraphernalia of a free and imaginative mind. The total effect is of chaos tidied in honour of an occasion, and of a temporary elegance created by the furniture borrowed from Harold Gorringe and arranged to its best advantage.

This consists of three elegant Regency chairs in gold leaf; a Regency chaise-longue to match; a small Queen Anne table bearing a fine opaline lamp, with a silk shade; a Wedgewood bowl in black basalt; a good Coalport vase containing summer flowers, and a fine porcelain Buddha.

The only things which actually belong to Brindsley are a cheap square table bearing the drinks; an equally cheap round table in the middle of the room, shrouded by a cloth and decorated with the Wedgewood bowl; a low stool Downstage Centre, improved by the Buddha; a record player; a waste-paper basket; two or three large boxes by the door gaily decorated, and his own artistic creations. These are largely assumed to be in the studio awaiting inspection: but two of them are visible in this room. Upstage stands a bizarre iron sculpture dominated by two long detachable metal prongs; and, to the right, on a dais, stands another, hung with metal pieces which jangle loudly if touched. On the wall hang paintings, some of them presumably by Clea. All are non-figurative; colourful geometric designs, splashes, splodges and splats of colour; whirls and whorls and wiggles—all testifying more to a delight in handling paint than to an ability to achieve very much with it.

## THE TIME

Nine-thirty on a Sunday night.

## THE LIGHT

On the few occasions when a lighter is lit, matches are stuck or a torch is put on, the light on Stage merely gets dimmer. When these objects are extinguished, the Stage immediately grows brighter.

Before the Curtain goes up, house-lights should go down to half. The first blunt phrase of "The Stars and Stripes" only, is heard very loud on the front-of-house speakers. Then it, and the house lights snap off together. Curtain rises in darkness.

## NOTE FOR HAROLD IN THE FURNITURE-MOVING SCENE

In speaking his monologue, "Well, I'd just opened up" etc., page 77, et seq., Harold must never struggle to make his lines heard above audience laughter, or pause for it to stop. He must subordinate his words entirely to the laughter evoked by Brindsley's struggle with the furniture, and keep on talking through it.

# Black Comedy

AT RISE: *COMPLETE DARKNESS. Two voices are heard:* BRINDSLEY *and* CAROL. *They must give the impression of two people walking round a room with absolute confidence, as if in the light. A chair is put down hard.*

BRINDSLEY. There! How do you think the room looks?

CAROL. (*Quacking.*) Fabulous! I wish we could always see it like this. That lamp looks divine there. And those chairs are just the right colour. I told you green would look well in here.

BRINDSLEY. Suppose Harold comes back?

CAROL. He is not coming back till tomorrow morning.

BRINDSLEY. (*He paces nervously.*) I know. But suppose he comes back tonight? He's mad about his antiques. What do you think he'll say if he goes into his room and finds out we've stolen them?

CAROL. Don't dramatize. We haven't stolen all his furniture. Just three chairs, the sofa, that table, the lamp, the bowl and the vase of flowers, that's all.

BRINDSLEY. And the Buddha. That's more valuable than anything.

CAROL. Oh, do stop worrying, darling.

BRINDSLEY. Well, you don't know Harold. He won't even let anyone touch his antiques.

CAROL. Look, we'll put everything back as soon as Mr. Bamberger leaves. Now stop being dreary.

BRINDSLEY. Well, frankly, I don't think we should have done it. I mean—*anyway*, Harold or no.

CAROL. Why not, for heaven's sake? The room looks divine now. Just look at it!

BRINDSLEY. Darling, Georg Bamberger's a multimillionaire. He's lived all his life against this sort of furniture. Our few stolen bits aren't going to impress him. He's coming to see the work of an unknown sculptor. If you ask me, it would look much better to him if he found me exactly as I really am: a poor artist. It might touch his heart.

CAROL. It might—but it certainly won't impress Daddy. Remember he's coming too.

BRINDSLEY. As if I could forget! Why you had to invite your monster father tonight, I can't think!

CAROL. Oh, not again!

BRINDSLEY. Well, it's too bloody much. If he's going to be persuaded I'm a fit husband for you, just by watching a famous collector buy some of my work, he doesn't deserve to have me as a son-in-law!

CAROL. He just wants some proof you can earn your own living.

BRINDSLEY. And what if Bamberger *doesn't* like my work?

CAROL. He will, darling. Just stop worrying.

BRINDSLEY. I can't. Get me a whiskey. (*She does. We hear her steps, and a GLASS clink against a bottle.*) I've got a foreboding. It's all going to be a disaster. An A-one, copper-bottomed, twenty-four-carat disaster.

CAROL. Look, darling, you know what they say. Faint heart never won fair ladypegs!

BRINDSLEY. How true.

CAROL. The trouble with you is you're what Daddy calls a Determined Defeatist.

BRINDSLEY. The more I hear about your Daddy, the more I hate him. I loathe military men, anyway . . . and in any case, he's bound to hate me.

CAROL. Why?

BRINDSLEY. Because I'm a complete physical coward. He'll smell it on my breath. (*He sits on the sofa.*)

CAROL. Look, darling, all you've got to do is stand up to him. Daddy's only a bully when he thinks people are afraid of him.

BRINDSLEY. Well, I am.

CAROL. You haven't even met him.

BRINDSLEY. That doesn't make any difference.

CAROL. Don't be ridiculous. (*Hands him a drink.*) Here.

BRINDSLEY. Thanks.

CAROL. What can he do? To you?

BRINDSLEY. For one thing, he can refuse to let me marry you.

CAROL. Ah, that's sweet.

(*They embrace.*)

BRINDSLEY. I like you in yellow. It brings out your hair.

CAROL. Straighten your tie. You look sloppypegs.

BRINDSLEY. Well, you look divine.

CAROL. Really?

BRINDSLEY. I mean it. I've never seen you look so lovely.

CAROL. Tell me, Brin, have there been many before me?

BRINDSLEY. Thousands.

CAROL. Seriously.

BRINDSLEY. Seriously—none.

CAROL. What about that girl in the photo?

BRINDSLEY. She lasted about three months.

CAROL. When?

BRINDSLEY. Two years ago.

CAROL. What was her name?

BRINDSLEY. Clea.

CAROL. What was she like?

BRINDSLEY. She was a painter. Very honest. Very clever. And just about as cozy as a steel razor-blade.

CAROL. When was the last time you saw her?

BRINDSLEY. (*Evasively.*) I told you . . . two years ago.

CAROL. Well, why did you still have her photo in your bedroom drawer?

BRINDSLEY. It was just there, that's all. Give me a kiss . . . No one in the world kisses like you.

CAROL. (*Murmuring.*) Tell me something . . . did you like it better with her—or me?

BRINDSLEY. Like what?

CAROL. Sexipegs.

BRINDSLEY. Look, people will be here in a minute. Put a record on. It had better be something for your father. What does he like?

CAROL. (*Crossing to the record player.*) He doesn't like anything except military marches.

BRINDSLEY. I might have guessed . . . Wait,—I think I've got some! That last record on the shelf. The orange cover. It's called "Marching and Murdering with Sousa," or something.

CAROL. This one?

BRINDSLEY. That's it.

CAROL. (*Getting it.*) "The Band of the Coldstream Guards."

BRINDSLEY. Ideal. Put it on.

CAROL. How d'you switch on?

BRINDSLEY. The last knob on the left. That's it . . . Let us pray! Oh God, let this evening go all right! Let Mr. Bamberger like my sculpture and buy some! Let Carol's monster father like me! And let my neighbour Harold Gorringe never find out that we borrowed his precious furniture behind his back! Amen. (*A Sousa MARCH; loud. Hardly has it begun, however, when it RUNS DOWN—as if there is a failure of electricity. Brilliant LIGHT floods the Stage. The rest of the play, save for the times when matches are struck, or for the scene with* SCHUPPANZIGH, *is acted in this light, but as if in pitch darkness. They freeze:* CAROL *by the end of the sofa;* BRINDSLEY *by the drinks table. The* GIRL'S *dress is a silk flag of chic wrapped round her greyhound's body. The* BOY'S *look is equally cool: narrow, contained, and sexy. Throughout the evening, as things slide into disaster for him, his crisp, detached shape degenerates progressively into sweat and rumple,—just as the elegance of his room gives way relentlessly to its usual near-slum appearance. For the place, as for its owner, the evening is a progress through disintegration.*) Blast! A fuse!

CAROL. *Oh, no!*

BRINDSLEY. It must be. (*He blunders to the light switch, feeling ahead of him, trying to part the darkness with his hands. Finding the switch, he flicks it on and off.*)

CAROL. It is!

BRINDSLEY. Oh, no!

CAROL. Or a power cut. Where's the box?

BRINDSLEY. In the hall.

CAROL. Have you any candles?

BRINDSLEY. No. Damn!

CAROL. Where are the matches?

BRINDSLEY. They should be on the drinks table. (*Feeling round the bottles.*) No. Try on the record player. (*They both start groping about the room, feeling for matches.*) Damn, damn, damn, damn, damn, damn!

CAROL. (*She slides a maracca rattling off the record player.*) There! (*Finding it.*) No . . .

(*The TELEPHONE rings.*)

BRINDSLEY. Would you believe it?! (*He blunders his way towards the sound of the bell. Just in time he remembers the central table—and stops himself colliding into it with a smile of self-congratulation.*) All right: I'm coming! (*Instead he trips over the dais, and goes sprawling—knocking the phone onto the floor. He has to grope for it on his knees, hauling receiver back to him by the wire. Into receiver.*) Hallo? . . . (*In sudden horror.*) Hallo! . . . No, no, no, no—I'm fine, just fine! . . . You! . . . (*His hand over the receiver: to* CAROL.) Darling—look in the bedroom, will you?

CAROL. I haven't finished in here yet.

BRINDSLEY. Well, I've just remembered there's some

fuse wire in the bedroom. In that drawer where you found the photograph. Go and get it, will you?

CAROL. I don't think there is. I didn't see any there.

BRINDSLEY. (*Snapping.*) Don't argue. Just look!

CAROL. All right. Keep your hairpiece on. (*During the following she gropes her way cautiously up the stairs— head down, arms up the bannisters, silken bottom thrust out with the effort.*)

BRINDSLEY. (*Controlling himself.*) I'm sorry. I just know it's there, that's all. You must have missed it.

CAROL. What about the matches?

BRINDSLEY. We'll have to mend it in the dark, that's all. Please hurry, dear.

CAROL. (*Climbing.*) Oh God, how dreary! (*She reaches the top of the stairs—and from force of habit pulls down her skirt before groping her way into the bedroom.*)

BRINDSLEY. (*Hand still over the receiver.*) Carol? . . . Darling? . . . (*Satisfied she has gone; in a rush into the telephone, his voice low.*) Clea! What are you doing here? I thought you were in Finland . . . But you've hardly been gone six weeks . . . Where are you speaking from? . . . The Air Terminal? . . . Well, no,—that's not a good idea tonight. I'm terribly busy, and I'm afraid I just can't get out of it. It's business.

CAROL. (*Calling from the bedroom, above.*) There's nothing here except your dreary socks. I told you.

BRINDSLEY. (*Calling back.*) Well, try the other drawers . . . (*He rises as he speaks, turning so that the wire wraps itself around his legs. CAROL returns to her search. Low and rapid, into phone.*) Look: I can't stop now. Can I call you tomorrow? Where will you be? . . . Look, I told you *no*, Clea. Not tonight. I know it's just around the corner, that's not the point. You can't come round . . . Look, the situation's changed . . . Something's happened this past month—

CAROL. I can't see anything. Brin, *please!*—

BRINDSLEY. Clea, I've got to go . . . Look, I can't

discuss it over the phone . . . Has it got to do with what? Yes, of course it has. I mean you can't expect things to stay frozen, can you?

CAROL. (*Emerging from the bedroom.*) There's nothing here. Haven't we any matches at all?

BRINDSLEY. Oh stop wailing! (*Into phone.*) No, not you! I'll call you tomorrow. Goodbye. (*He hangs up sharply—but fails to find the rest of the telephone, so that he bangs the receiver hard on the table first. Then he has to disentangle himself from the wire. Already* BRINDSLEY *is beginning to be fussed.*)

CAROL. (*Descending.*) Who was that?

BRINDSLEY. Just a chum. Did you find the wire?

CAROL. I can't find anything in this. We've *got* to get some matches!—

BRINDSLEY. I'll try the pub. Perhaps they'll have some candles as well.

(*Little screams are heard approaching from above. It is* MISS FURNIVAL *groping her way down in a panic.*)

MISS FURNIVAL. (*Squealing.*) Help! Help! . . . Oh please, someone help me! . . .

BRINDSLEY. (*Calling out.*) Is that you, Miss Furnival?

MISS FURNIVAL. Mr. Miller? . . .

BRINDSLEY. Yes?

MISS FURNIVAL. Mr. Miller!

BRINDSLEY. Yes!

(*She gropes her way in.* BRINDSLEY *crosses to find her, but narrowly misses her. She carries a handbag.*)

MISS FURNIVAL. Oh, thank God, you're there; I'm so frightened! . . .

BRINDSLEY. Why? Have your lights gone too?

MISS FURNIVAL. Yes!

BRINDSLEY. It must be a power cut. (*He finds her hand and leads her to the chair Downstage Left. Then he sits in it himself first, pulls her gently towards him backwards by the waist, and slides out from under as she sits on it.*)

MISS FURNIVAL. I don't think so. The street lights are on in the front. I saw them from the landing.

BRINDSLEY. Then it must be the mains switch of the house.

CAROL. Where is that?

(MISS FURNIVAL *gasps at the strange voice.*)

BRINDSLEY. Down in the cellar. It's all sealed up. No one's allowed to touch it but the electricity people.

CAROL. What are we going to do?

BRINDSLEY. Get them—quick!

CAROL. Will they come at this time of night?

BRINDSLEY. They've got to. (BRINDSLEY *accidentally touches* MISS FURNIVAL's *breasts. She gives a little scream. Groping his way to the phone.*) Have you by any chance got a match on you, Miss Furnival?

MISS FURNIVAL. I'm afraid I haven't. So improvident of me. And I'm absolutely terrified of the dark.

BRINDSLEY. Darling, this is Miss Furnival, from upstairs. Miss Furnival—Miss Melkett.

MISS FURNIVAL. How do you do?

CAROL. How do you do?

MISS FURNIVAL. Isn't this frightful?

(BRINDSLEY *picks up the phone and dials "O."*)

CAROL. Perhaps we can put Mr. Bamberger off.

BRINDSLEY. Impossible. He's dining out and coming on here after. He can't be reached.

CAROL. Oh, flip!

BRINDSLEY. (*Sitting on the dais, and speaking into the phone.*) Hullo, Operator, can you give me the London Electricity Board, please? Night Service . . . I'm sure it's in the book, Miss, but I'm afraid I can't see . . . There's no need to apologise. No, I'm not blind!—I just can't see: we've got a fuse . . . (*Desperate.*) Miss, *please:* this is an emergency . . . Thank you! . . . (*To the room.*) London is staffed with imbeciles!

MISS FURNIVAL. Oh, you're so right, Mr. Miller.

BRINDSLEY. (*Rising, frantic: into the phone.*) Miss, I *don't want* the number: I can't dial it! . . . Well, have *you* ever tried to dial a number in the dark? . . . (*Trying to keep control.*) I just want to be connected . . . Thank you . . . (*To* MISS FURNIVAL.) Miss Furnival, do you by any remote chance have any candles?

MISS FURVINAL. I'm afraid not, Mr. Miller.

BRINDSLEY. (*Mouthing nastily at her.*) "I'm afraid not, Mr. Miller" . . . (*Briskly, into phone.*) Hello? Look, I'd like to report mains fuse at Eighteen Scarlatti Gardens. My name is Miller. (*Exasperated.*) Yes, yes! All right! . . . (*Maddened: to the room.*) Hold on! Hold bloody on! . . .

MISS FURNIVAL. If I might suggest—Harold Gorringe opposite might have some candles. He's away for the week end, but always leaves his key under the mat.

BRINDSLEY. Good idea. That's just the sort of practical thing he would have. (*To* CAROL.) Here—take this . . . I'll go and see, love. (*He moves to hand her the telephone —but the wire goes taut between his legs, so that the base of the phone catches him in the groin. He gasps.* CAROL *takes the phone.*)

MISS FURNIVAL. Are you all right, Mr. Miller?

BRINDSLEY. (*Hopping to the door.*) I knew it! I bloody knew it. This is going to be the worst night of my life! . . . (*He collides with the door.*)

CAROL. Don't panic, darling. Just don't panic!

(*He stumbles out, and is seen groping under* HAROLD's *mat for the key. He finds it and enters the room opposite.*)

MISS FURNIVAL. You're so right, Miss Melkett. We must none of us panic.

CAROL. (*On the phone.*) Hallo? Hallo? (*To* MISS FURNIVAL.) This would have to happen tonight. It's just Brindsley's luck.

MISS FURNIVAL. Is it something special tonight then, Miss Melkett?

CAROL. It couldn't be something more special if it tried.

MISS FURNIVAL. Oh, dear. May I ask why?

CAROL. Have you ever heard of a German called Georg Bamberger?

MISS FURNIVAL. Indeed, yes. Isn't he the richest man in the world?

CAROL. Yes. (*Into phone.*) Hallo? . . . (*To* MISS FURNIVAL.) Well, he's coming here tonight.

MISS FURNIVAL. Tonight!

CAROL. In about twenty minutes, to be exact. And to make matters worse, he's apparently stone deaf . . .

MISS FURNIVAL. How extraordinary! May I ask why he's coming?

CAROL. He saw some photos of Brindsley's work, and apparently got madly excited about it. His secretary rang up last week and asked if he could come and see it. He's a great collector. Brin would be absolutely *made* if Bamberger bought a piece of his.

MISS FURNIVAL. Oh, how exciting!

CAROL. It's his big break. Or was—till a moment ago.

MISS FURNIVAL. Oh my dear, you *must* get some help. Jiggle that thing.

CAROL. (*Jiggling the phone.*) *Hallo? Hallo?* . . . Perhaps the Bomb's fallen, and everyone's dead.

MISS FURNIVAL. Oh, please don't say things like that: —even in levity.

CAROL. (*Someone answers her at last.*) Hallo? Ah! This is Number Eighteen, Scarlatti Gardens. I'm afraid we've had the most dreary fuse. It's what's laughingly known as the Main Switch. We want a *little man* . . . Well, they can't all have flu . . . Oh, please try! It's screamingly urgent . . . Thank you. (*She hangs up.*) Sometime this evening, they hope. That's a lot of help.

MISS FURNIVAL. They're not here to help, my dear. In my young days you paid your rates and you got satisfaction. Nowadays you just get some foreigner swearing at you. And if they think you're of the middle class, that only makes it worse . . .

CAROL. Would you like a drink?

MISS FURNIVAL. I don't drink, thank you. My dear father, being a Baptist minister, strongly disapproved of alcohol.

(*A SCUFFLE is heard amongst milk bottles off, followed by a stifled oath.*)

COL. MELKETT. Damn and blast! (*Barking.*) Is there anybody there?

CAROL. (*Calling.*) In here, daddypegs!

COLONEL. Can't you put the light on, dammit? I've almost knocked meself out on a damn milk bottle.

CAROL. We've got a fuse. Nothing's working.

(COL. MELKETT *appears, in a bowler hat, carrying an umbrella, holding a lighter which evidently is working—we can see the flame, and of course, the LIGHTS go down a little.*)

MISS FURNIVAL. Oh, what a relief! A light!

CAROL. This is my father, Colonel Melkett, Miss Furnival. She's from upstairs.

COLONEL. Good evening.

MISS FURNIVAL. I'm taking refuge for a moment with Mr. Miller. I'm not very good in the dark.

COLONEL. When did this happen?

(MISS FURNIVAL, *glad for the light, follows it pathetically as the* COLONEL *crosses the room.*)

CAROL. Five minutes ago. The mains just blew.

COLONEL. And where's this young man of yours?

CAROL. In the flat opposite. He's trying to find candles.

COLONEL. You mean he hasn't got any?

CAROL. No. We can't even find the matches.

COLONEL. I see. No organization. Bad sign!

CAROL. Daddy, please. It could happen to any of us.

COLONEL. Not to me. (*He turns to find* MISS FURNIVAL *right behind him and glares at her balefully. The poor* WOMAN *retreats to the sofa and sits down.* COLONEL MELKETT *gets his first sight of* BRINDSLEY'S *sculpture.*) What the hell's that?

CAROL. Some of Brindsley's work.

COLONEL. Is it, by Jove? And how much does that cost?

CAROL. I think he's asking fifty pounds for it.

COLONEL. My God!

CAROL. (*Nervously.*) Do you like the flat, Daddy? He's furnished it very well, hasn't he? I mean it's rich, but not gaudipegs.

COLONEL. (*Seeing the Buddha.*) Very elegant—good: I can see he's got excellent taste. Now that's what I understand by a real work of art—you can see what it's meant to be.

MISS FURNIVAL. Good heavens!

CAROL. What is it?

MISS FURNIVAL. Nothing . . . It's just that Buddha—it so closely resembles the one Harold Gorringe has.

(CAROL *looks panic-stricken.*)

COLONEL. It must have cost a pretty penny, what? He must be quite well off . . .

CAROL. Well . . .

COLONEL. By Jove—it's got pretty colours. (*He bends to examine it.*)

CAROL. (*Sotto voce, urgently, to* MISS FURNIVAL.) You know Mr. Gorringe?

MISS FURNIVAL. Oh very well indeed. We're excellent friends. He has such lovely things . . . (*For the first time she notices the sofa on which she is sitting.*) Oh . . .

CAROL. What?

MISS FURNIVAL. This furniture . . . (*Looking about her.*) Surely—?—my goodness!—

CAROL. (*Hastily.*) Daddy, why don't you go in there? It's Brin's studio.

COLONEL. What for?

CAROL. You—you can leave your umbrella there.

COLONEL. Very well, Dumpling. Anythin' to oblige. (*To* MISS FURNIVAL.) Excuse me.

(*He goes off into the studio, taking his lighter with him. The LIGHT instantly gets brighter on Stage.* CAROL *sits beside the* SPINSTER *on the sofa, crouching like a conspirator.*)

CAROL. (*Low and urgent.*) Miss Furnival, you're a sport, aren't you?

MISS FURNIVAL. I don't know. What is this furniture doing in here? It belongs to Harold Gorringe.

CAROL. I know. We've done something absolutely frightful. We've stolen all his best pieces and put Brin's horrid old bits into *his* room.

MISS FURNIVAL. But why? It's disgraceful!

CAROL. (*Sentimentally.*) Because Brindsley's got nothing, Miss Furnival. Nothing at all. He's as poor as a church mouse. If Daddy had seen this place as it looks normally, he'd have forbidden our marriage on the spot . . . Mr. Gorringe wasn't there to ask—so we just took the chance.

MISS FURNIVAL. If Harold Gorringe knew that anyone had touched his furniture or his porcelain, he'd go out of his mind! And as for that Buddha— (*Points in the wrong direction.*) it's the most precious piece he owns. It's worth hundreds of pounds.

CAROL. Oh, please, Miss Furnival—you won't give us away, will you? We're desperate . . . And it's only for an hour . . . Oh, please! *please!*

MISS FURNIVAL. (*Giggling.*) Very well! I won't betray you!

CAROL. Oh, thank you!

MISS FURNIVAL. But it'll have to go back exactly as it was, just as soon as Mr. Bamberger and your father leave.

CAROL. I swear! Oh, Miss Furnival, you're an angel!
. . . Do have a drink. Oh no, you don't. Well, have a
bitter lemon.
MISS FURNIVAL. Thank you. That I won't refuse.

(*The* COLONEL *returns, hatless but still holding his lighter.
Stage darkens a little.*)

COLONEL. Well! That's supposed to be sculpture?
CAROL. It's not supposed to be. It is.
COLONEL. They'd make good garden implements. I'd
like 'em for turnin' the soil.

(MISS FURNIVAL *giggles.*)

CAROL. That's not very funny, Daddy.

(MISS FURNIVAL *stops giggling.*)

COLONEL. Sorry, Dumpling. Speak as you find.
CAROL. I wish you wouldn't call me Dumpling.
COLONEL. Well, there's no point wastin' this. We may
need it! (*He snaps off his lighter.*)

(MISS FURNIVAL *gives her little gasp as Stage brightens.*)

CAROL. Don't be nervous, Miss Furnival. Brin will be
here in a minute with the candles.
MISS FURNIVAL. Then I'll leave, of course. I don't want
to be in your way.
CAROL. You're not at all. (*Hearing him.*) Brin?—

(BRINDSLEY *comes out of* HAROLD'S *room—returns the
key under the mat.*)

BRINDSLEY. Hello?
CAROL. Did you find anything?
BRINDSLEY. (*Coming in.*) You can't find anything in

this. If there's candles there, *I* don't know where they are. Did you get the electric people?

CAROL. They said they might send someone around later.

BRINDSLEY. How much later?

CAROL. They don't now.

BRINDSLEY. That's a lot of help. What a lookout! Not a bloody candle in the house. A deaf millionaire to show sculpture to—and your monster father to keep happy. Lovely!

COLONEL. (*Grimly lighting his lighter.*) Good evenin'.

(BRINDSLEY *jumps.*)

CAROL. Brin, this *is* my father—Colonel Melkett.

BRINDSLEY. (*Wildly embarrassed.*) Well, well, well, well, well! . . . (*Panic.*) Good evening, sir. Fancy you being there all the time! I—I'm expecting some dreadful neighbours, some neighbour monsters, monster neighbours, you know . . . They rang up and said they might look round . . . Well, well, well . . .

COLONEL. (*Darkly.*) Well, well.

MISS FURNIVAL. (*Nervously.*) Well, well . . .

CAROL. (*Brightly.*) Well!

(*The* COLONEL *rises and advances on* BRINDSLEY *who retreats before him across the room.*)

COLONEL. You seem to be in a spot of trouble.

BRINDSLEY. (*With mad nervousness.*) Oh, no no, no, no, no, no, *no!* Just a fuse—nothing really, we have them all the time . . . I mean, it won't be the first fuse I've survived, and it won't be the last, I suppose . . . (*He gives a wild braying laugh.*)

COLONEL. (*Relentless.*) In the meantime, you've got no matches. Right?

BRINDSLEY. Right.

COLONEL. No candles. Right?

BRINDSLEY. Right.

COLONEL. No basic efficiency, right?

BRINDSLEY. I wouldn't say that, exactly . . .

COLONEL. By basic efficiency, young man, I mean the simple state of being At Attention in life, rather than At Ease. Understand?

BRINDSLEY. Well, I'm certainly not at ease, sir.

COLONEL. What are you goin' to do about it?

BRINDSLEY. Do?

COLONEL. Don't echo me, sir. I don't like it.

BRINDSLEY. You don't like it. (*Realising that is another "echo."*) I'm sorry.

COLONEL. Now look you here. This is an emergency. Anyone can see that.

BRINDSLEY. No one can see anything: that's the emergency. (*He gives his braying laugh again.*)

COLONEL. Spare me your humour, sir, if you don't mind. Let's look at the situation objectively. Right?

BRINDSLEY. Right.

COLONEL. Good. (*He snaps off the lighter.*) Problem: Darkness. Solution: Light.

BRINDSLEY. Oh very good, sir.

COLONEL. Weapons: Matches: none. Candles: none. What remains?

BRINDSLEY. Search me.

COLONEL. (*Triumphantly.*) Torches. Torches, sir! what?

BRINDSLEY. Or a set of early Christians.

COLONEL. What did you say?

BRINDSLEY. I'm sorry. I think I'm becoming unhinged. Very good. Torches—brilliant.

COLONEL. Routine. Well, where would you find one?

BRINDSLEY. The pub. What time is it?

(*The* COLONEL *lights his lighter, but now not at the first try. The Stage LIGHT flickers up and down accordingly.*)

COLONEL. Blasted thing. It's beginnin' to go. (*He con-*

*sults his watch.*) Quarter to ten. You can just make it, if you hurry.

BRINDSLEY. Thank you, sir. Your clarity of mind has saved the day.

COLONEL. Well, get on with it, man.

BRINDSLEY. Yes, sir! Back in a minute.

(*The* COLONEL *sits in the Regency chair, Downstage Right, snapping off his lighter.* BRINDSLEY *makes an obscene gesture at him.*)

CAROL. Good luck, darling.

BRINDSLEY. Thank you, my sweet.

(*She blows him a kiss. He blows her one back.*)

COLONEL. (*Irritated.*) Stop that at once.

(BRINDSLEY *starts for the door—but as he reaches it,* HAROLD GORRINGE *is heard, off.*)

HAROLD. (*Broad Lancashire accent.*) Hallo? Hallo? Anyone there?

BRINDSLEY. (*Freezing with horror.*) HAROLD!!

HAROLD. Brindsley?

BRINDSLEY. (*Meant for* CAROL.) It's Harold. He's back!

CAROL. Oh, no!

BRINDSLEY. THE FURNITURE!!

HAROLD. What's going on here? (HAROLD *appears, in modish suit and flowered shirt. Over his shoulders he wears a smart raincoat [or cape] and carries a week-end bag. His hair falls over his brow in a flossy attempt at elegance.*)

BRINDSLEY. Nothing, Harold. Don't go in there! . . . The mains have fused. It's dark—it's all over the house.

HAROLD. Have you phoned the electric? (*Reaching out.*)

BRINDSLEY. Yes. Come in here. (*Grabs him.*)

HAROLD. Oh! . . . It's rather camp in the dark, isn't it?

BRINDSLEY. (*Desperately.*) Yes, I suppose so! . . . So you're back from your week-end, then!

HAROLD. I certainly am, dear. Week-end! Some week-end! It rained the whole bloody time. I'm damp to my panties.

BRINDSLEY. (*Nervously.*) Well, have a drink, then, and tell *us* all about it.

HAROLD. Us? Who's here, then?

MISS FURNIVAL. (*Archly.*) I am, Mr. Gorringe.

HAROLD. Ferny?

MISS FURNIVAL. Taking refuge, I'm afraid. You know how I hate the dark.

COLONEL. (*Attempting to light his lighter.*) Blasted thing! . . . (*He succeeds.*) There we are! (*Raising it to* GORRINGE'S *face, with distaste.*) Who are you?

BRINDSLEY. May I present my neighbour? This is Harold Gorringe—Colonel Melkett.

HAROLD. How do?

COLONEL. How d'ye do?

BRINDSLEY. And this is Miss Carol Melkett, Harold Gorringe.

CAROL. (*Giving him a chilly smile.*) Hallo!

(HAROLD *nods coldly.* BRINDSLEY *neatly strips the raincoat off his back, and drops it adroitly over the Wedgwood bowl on the table.* HAROLD *turns in surprise.*)

COLONEL. You've got no candles, I suppose?

HAROLD. Would you believe it, Colonel, but I haven't? Silly me!

(BRINDSLEY *crosses and blows out the* COLONEL'S *lighter, just as* HAROLD *begins to look round the room. The Stage brightens.*)

COLONEL. What the devil did you do that for?

BRINDSLEY. I'm saving your wick, Colonel. You may need it later and it's failing fast.

(*The* COLONEL *gives him a suspicious look.* BRINDSLEY *moves quickly back, takes up the coat and drops it over the Right end of the sofa, to conceal as much of it as possible.*)

HAROLD. It's all right. I've got some matches.

CAROL. (*Alarmed.*) Matches!

HAROLD. Here we are! I hope I've got the right end. (*He strikes one.* BRINDSLEY *immediately blows it out from behind, then moves swiftly to hide the Wedgewood bowl under the table, and drop the table-cloth over the remaining end of the sofa.* MISS FURNIVAL *sits serenely unknowing between the two covers.*) Hey, what was that?

BRINDSLEY. (*Babbling.*) A draught. No match stays alight in this room. It's impossible. Cross-currents, you know. Old houses are full of them. They're almost a permanent feature in this house . . .

HAROLD. (*Bewildered.*) I don't know what you're on about. (*He strikes another match.* BRINDSLEY *again blows it out as he nips over to sit in the chair Downstage Left, but this time is seen.*) What's up with you?

BRINDSLEY. Nothing!

HAROLD. Have you got a dead body in here or something?

BRINDSLEY. NO! (*He starts his maniacal laughter.*)

HAROLD. Here, have you been drinking?

BRINDSLEY. No. Of course not!!

(HAROLD *strikes another match.* BRINDSLEY *leaps up, and blows it out. All these strikings and blowings are of course accompanied by swift and violent alterations of the LIGHT.*)

HAROLD. (*Exasperated.*) Now look here! What's up with you?

BRINDSLEY. (*Inspired.*) Dangerous!

HAROLD. What?

BRINDSLEY. (*Frantically improvising.*) Dangerous! It's dangerous! . . . We can all die! Naked flames! Hideous accidents can happen with naked flames! . . .

HAROLD. I don't know what you're on about!

BRINDSLEY. I've just remembered! It's something they always warn you about. In old houses the fuse box and the gas meter are in the same cupboard. They are here!

COLONEL. So what about it?

BRINDSLEY. Well . . . electrical blowouts can damage the gas supply. They're famous for it. They do it all the time! And you've got to avoid naked flames till they're mended.

COLONEL. I've never heard of that.

HAROLD. Me neither.

BRINDSLEY. (*Leading HAROLD gently to the sofa. HAROLD sits.*) Well, take my word for it. It's fantastically dangerous to burn a naked flame in this room!

CAROL. (*Catching on.*) Brin's absolutely right. In fact, they warned me about it on the phone this evening when I called them. They said, "Whatever you do, don't strike a match till the fuse is mended."

BRINDSLEY. There, you see!—it's terribly dangerous.

COLONEL. (*Grimly.*) Then why didn't you warn me, Dumpling?

CAROL. I—I forgot.

COLONEL. Brilliant!

MISS FURNIVAL. Oh goodness, we must take care.

BRINDSLEY. We certainly must! (*Pause.*) Let's all have a drink. Cheer us up!

CAROL. Good idea! Mr. Gorringe, would you like a drink?

HAROLD. Well, I must say, that wouldn't come amiss. Not after the journey I've had tonight. I swear to God there was thirty-five people in that compartment if there was one—babes in arms, toddlers, two nuns, three yapping poodles, and not a sausage to eat from Leamington to London. It's a bloody disgrace.

MISS FURNIVAL. You'd think they'd put on a restaurant car, Mr. Gorringe.

HAROLD. Not them, Ferny. They don't care if you perish once they've got your fare. Excuse me, I'll just go and clean up.

BRINDSLEY. (*Panic.*) You can do that here.

HAROLD. Well, I must unpack anyway. (*He rises, taking* MISS FURNIVAL'S *handbag instead of his own week-end bag. It hangs from his wrist.*)

BRINDSLEY. Do it later.

HAROLD. No, I hate to keep clothes in a suitcase longer than I absolutely have to. If there's one thing I can't stand, it's a creased suit.

BRINDSLEY. (*Pushing him back on to the sofa.*) Five more minutes won't hurt, surely?

HAROLD. (*Pleased.*) Ooh, you aren't half bossy.

CAROL. What will you have? Winnie, Vera or Ginette?

HAROLD. Come again.

CAROL. Winnie Whiskey, Vera Vodka, or dear old standby Ginette.

HAROLD. (*Yielding.*) I can see you're the camp one! . . . If it's all the same to you, I'll have a drop of Ginette, please, and a little lime juice.

COLONEL. Young man, do I have to keep reminding you that you are in an emergency? You have a guest arrivin' any second.

BRINDSLEY. Oh God, I'd forgotten!

COLONEL. Try the pub. Try the neighbours. Try who you damn well please, sir—but *get a torch!*

BRINDSLEY. Yes . . . Yes! . . . (*Casually.*) Carol, can I have a word with you, please?

CAROL. I'm here. (*She gropes towards him and* BRINDS-LEY *leads her to the stairs.*)

COLONEL. What now?

BRINDSLEY. Excuse us just a moment, please, Colonel. (*He pulls her quickly after him, up the stairs.*)

MISS FURNIVAL. (*As they do this.*) Oh, Mr. Gorringe, it's so exciting. You'll never guess who's coming here to-night.

HAROLD. Who?

MISS FURNIVAL. Guess.

HAROLD. The Queen!

MISS FURNIVAL. Oh, Mr. Gorringe, you are ridiculous!

(BRINDSLEY, *arriving at the top of the stairs, then opens the bedroom door and closes it behind them.*)

BRINDSLEY. What are we going to do?

CAROL. I don't know!

BRINDSLEY. Think!

CAROL. But—

BRINDSLEY. *Think!*

COLONEL. Is that boy touched or somethin'?

HAROLD. Touched? He's an absolute poppet.

COLONEL. A what?

HAROLD. A duck. I've known him for years, ever since he came here. There's not many secrets we keep from each other, I can tell you.

COLONEL. (*Frostily.*) Really?

HAROLD. Yes, really. He's a very sweet boy.

BRINDSLEY. We'll have to put all Harold's furniture back in his room.

CAROL. *Now?*

BRINDSLEY. We'll have to. I can't get a torch till we do.

CAROL. We can't!

BRINDSLEY. We must. He'll go mad if he finds out what we've done.

HAROLD. Well come on, Ferny: don't be a tease. Who is it? Who's coming?

MISS FURNIVAL. I'll give you a clue. It's someone with money.

HAROLD. Money? . . . Let me think.

COLONEL. (*Calling out.*) Carol!

CAROL. Look, can't you just tell him it was a joke?

BRINDSLEY. You don't know him. He can't bear any-one to touch his treasures. They're like children to him. He cleans everything twice a day with a special swans-down duster. He'd wreck everything. Would you like him to call me a thief in front of your father?

CAROL. Of course not!

BRINDSLEY. Well, he would. He gets absolutely hys-terical. I've seen him.

COLONEL. (*Mildly.*) Brindsley!

CAROL. Well, how the hell can we do it?

HAROLD. It's no good. You can't hear up there.

BRINDSLEY. (*Stripping off his jacket.*) Look, you hold the fort. Serve them drinks. Just keep things going in the dark. Leave it all to me. I'll try and put everything back.

CAROL. It won't work.

BRINDSLEY. It's *got* to!

COLONEL. (*Roaring.*) *Brindsley!*

BRINDSLEY. (*Dashing to the door.*) Coming, sir . . . (*With false calm.*) I'm just getting some empties to take to the pub.

COLONEL. Say what you like. That boy's touched.

BRINDSLEY. (*To* CAROL, *intimately.*) Trust me, darling. (*They kiss.*)

COLONEL. At the double, Miller.

BRINDSLEY. Yes, sir! Yes, sir! (*In his anxiety, he misses his footing and falls neatly down the entire flight of stairs. Picking himself up.*) I'm off now, Colonel! Help is definitely on the way.

COLONEL. Well, hurry it up, man.

BRINDSLEY. Carol will give you drinks. If Mr. Bam-berger arrives, just explain the situation to him.

HAROLD. (*Feeling for his hand.*) Would you like me to come with you?

BRINDSLEY. No, no, no—good heavens: stay and enjoy yourself. (HAROLD *kisses his hand.* BRINDSLEY *pulls it away.*) I mean, you must be exhausted after all those poodles. A nice gin and lime will do wonders. I shan't be a minute. (*He reaches the door, opens it, then slams it loudly, remaining on the inside. Then he stealthily opens it again, stands dead still for a moment at Centre, silently indicating to himself the position of the chairs he has to move—quickly removes his shoes, puts them under the drinks-table—then finds his way to the first of the Regency chairs, Downstage Left, which he lifts noiselessly.*)

CAROL. (*With bright desperation.*) Well now, drinks! What's everyone going to have? . . . It's Ginette for Mr. Gorringe and I suppose Winnie for Daddy.

COLONEL. And how on earth are you going to do that in the dark?

CAROL. I remember the exact way I put out the bottles. It's very simple. (BRINDSLEY *bumps into her with the chair and she sits on it, squashing his foot.*)

HAROLD. Oh look, luv, let me strike a match. I'm sure it's not that dangerous, just for a minute. (*He strikes a mat h.*)

CAROL. Oh, no! . . . (BRINDSLEY *ducks down behind the chair, and he blows out the match.*) Do you want to blow us all up, Mr. Gorringe? . . . All poor Mr. Bamberger would find would be teensy weensy bits of us. Very messypegs.

(BRINDSLEY *steals out, Felix-the-cat-like, with the chair as* CAROL *fumblingly starts to mix drinks. He sets it down, opens* HAROLD's *door and disappears inside it with the chair.*)

HAROLD. Bamberger? Is that who's coming? Georg Bamberger?

MISS FURNIVAL. Yes. To see Mr. Miller's work. Isn't it exciting?

HAROLD. Well, I never! I read an article about him last week in the Sunday Mirror. He's known as the Mystery

Millionaire. He's almost completely deaf—deaf as a post—
and spends most of his time indoors alone with his collection. He hardly ever goes out, except to a gallery or a
private studio. That's the life! If I had money that's just
what *I'd* do. Collect all the china and porcelain I wanted.

(BRINDSLEY *returns with a poor, broken-down chair of
his own, and sets it down in the same position as the
one he has taken out. The second chair is harder.
It sits right across the room, Upstage Right. Deli-
cately he moves Downstage towards the Buddha—
switches direction just in time to avoid collision with
it—and instead is just about to walk into the* COLO-
NEL, *when he speaks.*)

MISS FURNIVAL. I've never met a millionaire. I've
always wondered if they feel different to us. I mean their
actual skins.

COLONEL. Their skins?

MISS FURNIVAL. Yes. I've always imagined they must
be softer than ours. Like the skins of young ladies when
I was a girl.

(BRINDSLEY, *startled, recoils on "their skins?"—and by
pure accident falls into the very chair he has been
looking for. He cannot believe his luck, as he joy-
fully identifies it, picks it up, and moves with it
eagerly towards the door, crossing two inches from*
MISS FURNIVAL'S *face staring smugly into the dark.
The dialogue continues without any pause.*)

COLONEL. What an interestin' idea.

HAROLD. Oh, she's very fanciful is our Ferny.

MISS FURNIVAL. Very kind of you, Mr. Gorringe.
You're always so generous with your compliments. (*As
she speaks this next speech,* BRINDSLEY *unfortunately
mis-aims, and carries the chair past the door, bumps into
the wall, retreats from it, and inadvertently shuts the door
softly with his back. Now he cannot get out of the room.*

*He has to set down the chair several paces behind him to the Right, find the door handle—his hands fly over the door like butterflies—turn it; then open the door; then re-find the chair which he has quite lost. He falls to his knees. His hands grope for it in ever-widening, ever more frantic circles, lightly brushing* HAROLD's *leg—who lightly scratches himself, automatically. At last he triumphs, and staggers from the room, nearly exhausted.*) But this is by no means fancy. In my day, softness of skin was quite the sign of refinement. Nowadays, of course, it's hard enough for us middle classes to keep ourselves decently clothed, let alone soft. My father used to say, even before the bombs came and burnt our dear little house at Wendover: "The game's up, my girl. We middle classes are as dead as the dodo." Poor Father, how right he was. (NOTE: *Hopefully, if this counterpoint of farce action goes well,* MISS FURNIVAL *may have to ab-lib a fair bit during all this, and not mind too much if nobody hears her. The essential thing for all four actors during the furniture moving is to preserve the look of ordinary conversation.*)

COLONEL. Your father was a professional man?

MISS FURNIVAL. He was a man of God, Colonel.

COLONEL. Oh. (BRINDSLEY *returns with a broken-down rocking chair of his own. He crosses gingerly to where the* COLONEL *is sitting and sets down the rocker immediately next to the* COLONEL's *chair.*) How are those drinks coming, Dumpling?

CAROL. Fine, Daddy. They'll be one minute.

COLONEL. Let me help you.

(BRINDSLEY, *behind the* COLONEL, *silently prays for him to get up.*)

CAROL. You can take this bitter lemon to Miss Furnival if you want.

COLONEL. Very well.

(*Finally he rises.* BRINDSLEY *immediately takes up his*

*chair. With his other hand* BRINDSLEY *pulls the rocker into the identical position. The* COLONEL *moves slowly across the room, arms outstretched for the bitter lemon. Unknowingly* BRINDSLEY *follows him, carrying the third Regency chair. The* COLONEL *collides gently with the table. At the same moment* BRINDSLEY *reaches it Upstage of him and searches for the Wedgwood bowl. Their hands narrowly miss. Then the* YOUNG MAN *remembers the bowl is under the table. Deftly he reaches down and retrieves it— and carrying it in one hand and the chair in the other, triumphantly leaves the room through the arch unconsciously provided by the outstretched arms of* CAROL *and the* COLONEL, *giving and receiving a glass of Scotch—which they think is lemonade.*)

CAROL. Here you are, Daddy. Bitter lemon for Miss Furnival.

COLONEL. Right you are, Dumpling. (*To* MISS FURNIVAL.) So your father was a minister then?

MISS FURNIVAL. He was a saint, Colonel. I'm only thankful he never lived to see the rudeness and vulgarity of life today.

(*The* COLONEL *sets off to find her but goes much too far to the Right.*)

HAROLD. (*He sits on the sofa beside her.*) Oooh, you're so right, Ferny. Rudeness and vulgarity—that's it to a T. The manners of some people today are beyond belief. Honestly. Did I tell you what happened in my shop last Friday? I don't think I did.

MISS FURNIVAL. No, Mr. Gorringe, I don't think so.

(*Her voice corrects the* COLONEL's *direction. During the following he tries to find her with the hand containing the glass.*)

HAROLD. Well, I'd just opened up—it was about quarter to ten and I was dusting off the teapots—you know,

Rockingham collects the dust something shocking!—when
who should walk in but that Mrs. Levitt, you know—the
ginger-haired bit I told you about, the one who thinks
she's God's gift to bachelors.

COLONEL. (*Finding her head with his other hand.*)
Here's your lemonade. (*He hands her the Scotch.*)

MISS FURNIVAL. Oh! . . . Thank you . . .

(*Throughout* HAROLD'S *story,* MISS FURNIVAL, *terrified,
nurses the glass, not drinking. The* COLONEL *finds his
way back to the chair he thinks he was sitting on before, which is now a rocker.*)

HAROLD. Anyway, she's got in her hand a vase I'd
sold her last week—it was a birthday present for an old
geezer she's having a bit of a ding dong somewhere in
Earls Court, hoping to collect all his lolly when he dies,
as I read the situation. I'm a pretty good judge of
character, Ferny, as you know—and she's a real grasper
if ever I saw one.

(*The* COLONEL *sits heavily in the rocking chair.*)

COLONEL. Dammit to hell!

CAROL. What's the matter, Daddy?

COLONEL. (*Unbelieving.*) It's a blasted rockin' chair!
I didn't see a blasted rockin' chair here before!

(BRINDSLEY *re-appears triumphantly carrying one of the
original Regency chairs he took out. He stands in the
room, a little below the doorway, for ten seconds—
then feels the chair all over—realises it's the wrong
one, and darts out again—to re-appear almost immediately with another of his own broken-down
wooden chairs, covered in paint, which he puts in
place of the second Regency chair, Upstage Right.*)

HAROLD. Oh yes, you want to watch that. It's in a

pretty ropey condition, I've told Brin about it several
times. Anyway, this vase.—I'd let her have it for twenty-
five pounds, and she'd got infinitely the best of the bar-
gain, no argument about that. (HAROLD *rises and leans
against the Centre table to tell his story more effectively*.)
Well, in she prances, her hair all done up in one of them
bouffon hair-dos, you know, tarty—French-like—it would
have looked fancy on a girl half her age with twice her
looks— (BRINDSLEY *mistakenly lifts the end of the sofa.*
MISS FURNIVAL *gives a little scream at the jolt*.) Exactly.
You know the sort. (BRINDSLEY *staggers in the opposite
direction Downstage onto the rostrum*.) And d'you know
what she says to me? "Mr. Gorringe," she says, "I've
been cheated."

MISS FURNIVAL. No!

HAROLD. Her very words. "Cheated." (BRINDSLEY
*collides with the sculpture on the dais. It jangles violently.
To it*.) Hush up, I'm talking!

CAROL. (*At the drinks table: Covering up*.) I'm fright-
fully sorry.

(*The heads of* HAROLD, *the* COLONEL, *and* MISS FURNIVAL
*all turn to her quickly at the same time, surprised,
then look back again at the sculpture*.)

HAROLD. Anyway—"Oh, I say, and how exactly has
that occurred, Mrs. Levitt?" "Well," she says, "quite by
chance I took this vase over to Bill Everett in the
Portobello, and he says it's not what you called it at all,
Chinese and very rare. He says it's a piece of nineteenth
century English trash." (BRINDSLEY *finds the lamp on
the Downstage table and picks it up. He walks with it
round the rocking chair, on which the* COLONEL *is now
sitting again*.) "Does he?" I say. "Does he?" I keep
calm. I always do when I'm riled. "Yes," she says. "He
does. And I'd thank you to give me money back."

(*The wire of the lamp has followed* BRINDSLEY *round*

*the bottom of the rocking chair. It catches.* BRINDS-
LEY *tugs it gently. The chair moves. Surprised, the*
COLONEL *jerks forward.* BRINDSLEY *tugs it again, and
then again, much harder. The rocking chair is pulled
forward, spilling the* COLONEL *out of it, onto the floor,
and then falling itself on top of him. The shade of
the lamp comes off. During the ensuing dialogue*
BRINDSLEY *gets to his knees and crawls right across
the room following the flex of the lamp. He finds the
plug, pulls it out, and—still on his knees—re-traces
his steps, winding up the wire around his arm, and
becoming helplessly entangled in it.* COLONEL *rights
the chair, but sits in a strange terror on the floor.*)

MISS FURNIVAL. How dreadful, Mr. Gorringe. What
did you do?

HAROLD. I counted to ten, and then I let her have it.
"In the first place," I said, "I don't expect my customers
to go checking up on my honesty behind my back. In
the second, Bill Everett is ignorant as Barnsley dirt, he
doesn't know Tang from Ting. And in the third place,
that applies to you, too, Mrs. Levitt."

MISS FURNIVAL. You didn't!

HAROLD. I certainly did—and worse than that. "You've
got in your hand," I said, "a minor masterpiece of
Chinese pottery. But in point of fact," I said, "you're
not even fit to hold a 1953 Coronation mug. Don't you
ever come in here again," I said, "—don't you cross my
threshold. Because if you do, Mrs. Levitt, I won't make
myself responsible for the consequences."

(BRINDSLEY *suddenly realises he has lost the shade. He
begins to search for it on his knees, crossing the
room.*)

CAROL. (*With two drinks in her hand.*) My, Mr.
Gorringe, how splendid of you. Here's your gin and lime.
You deserve it. (*She hands him the bitter lemon.*)

HAROLD. (*Accepting it.*) Ta. I was proper blazing, I didn't care.

CAROL. Where are you? Where are you, Daddy? Here's your Scotch.

COLONEL. (*Roaring in* BRINDSLEY's *face.*) Here I am, Dumpling!

(BRINDSLEY *darts away from him, collides with the table, then during the ensuing, moves on his knees in a rapid figure of eight between all the legs, as the* COLONEL *gets up dazedly, and fumbles his way to take the glass of gin and lime.*)

HAROLD. Carrotty old bitch—telling *me* about pottery!

MISS FURNIVAL. Do you care for porcelain yourself, Colonel?

COLONEL. I'm afraid I don't know very much about it, Madam—I like some of that Chinese stuff—you get some lovely colours, like on that statue I saw when I came in here—very delicate.

(BRINDSLEY *freezes.*)

HAROLD. What statue's that, Colonel?

COLONEL. The one on the packing case, sir. Very fine.

HAROLD. I didn't know Brin had any Chinese stuff. What's it of then?

CAROL. (*Covering up.*) Well, we've all got drinks, I'd like to propose Daddy's regimental toast. Raise your glasses, everyone! "To the dear old Twenty-Fifth Horse. Up the British, and Death to all Natives!"

MISS FURNIVAL. I'll drink to that!

HAROLD. Up the old Twenty-Fifth!

(*Quickly* BRINDSLEY *finds the Buddha; moves it from the packing-case to the table; then gets* HAROLD's *raincoat from the sofa, and wraps the statue up in it, leaving it on the table.*)

COLONEL. Thank you, Dumplin'. That was very touchin' of you. Very touchin' indeed. (*He swallows his drink.*) Dammit, that's gin!

HAROLD. I've got lemonade!

MISS FURNIVAL. Oh! Horrible! . . . Quite horrible! That would be alcohol, I suppose! . . . Oh dear, how unpleasant! (*Seizing her chance* MISS FURNIVAL *downs a huge draft of Scotch.*)

HAROLD. (*To* MISS FURNIVAL.) Here, luv, exchange with me. No—you get the lemonade—but I get the gin. Colonel—

COLONEL. Here, sir.

HAROLD. Here, Ferny.

(*The* COLONEL *hands her the gin and lime. He gets instead the bitter lemon from* HAROLD. HAROLD *gets the Scotch.*)

MISS FURNIVAL. Thank you.

HAROLD. Well, let's try again. Bottoms up!

COLONEL. Quite. (*They drink. Exhausted,* BRINDSLEY *finds the shade and holds it up in triumph. The* COLONEL *spits out his lemonade in a fury all over* BRINDSLEY, *who at this very moment is crawling toward him on his knees.*) Look here—I can't stand another minute of this. (*He fishes his lighter out of his pocket and angrily tries to light it.*)

CAROL. Daddy, please!

COLONEL. I don't care, Dumpling. If I blow us up, then I'll blow us up! This is ridiculous . . . (*His words die in the flame. He spies* BRINDSLEY *kneeling at his feet, wound about with lampwire.*) What the devil are you doin' there?

BRINDSLEY. (*Blowing out his lighter.*) Now don't be rash, Colonel. Isn't the first rule of an officer: "Don't involve your men in unnecessary danger"? (*Quickly he steals, still on his knees, to the table Downstage Right.*)

COLONEL. Don't be impertinent. Where's the torch?

BRINDSLEY. Er . . . the pub was closed.

HAROLD. You didn't go to the pub in that time, surely? You couldn't have done.

BRINDSLEY. Of course I did.

MISS FURNIVAL. But it's five streets away, Mr. Miller.

BRINDSLEY. Needs must when the devil drives, Miss Furnival. Whatever that means. (*Quickly he lifts the little table, and steals out of the room with it, and the wrecked lamp.*)

COLONEL. (*Who thinks he is still kneeling at his feet.*) Now look here: there's somethin' very peculiar goin' on in this room. I may not know about art, Miller, but I know men. I know a liar in the light, and I know one in the dark.

CAROL. Daddy!

COLONEL. I don't want to doubt your word, sir. All the same, I'd like your oath you went out to the public house. Well?

CAROL. (*Realizing he isn't there, raising her voice.*) Brin, Daddy's talking to you!

COLONEL. What are you shoutin' for?

BRINDSLEY. (*Rushing back from Harold's room, still entangled in the lamp.*) Of course. I know. He's absolutely right. I was—just thinking it over for a moment.

COLONEL. Well? What's your answer?

BRINDSLEY. I . . . I couldn't agree with you more, sir.

COLONEL. What?

BRINDSLEY. It was a very perceptive remark you made. Not everyone would have thought of that. Individual. You know. Almost witty.

COLONEL. Look, young man, are you trying to be funny?

BRINDSLEY. (*Ingratiatingly.*) Well, I'll try anything once! (*He dumps the broken lamp, wire and all, into the waste-paper basket, Upstage of the dais.*)

HAROLD. I say, this is becoming a bit unpleasant, isn't it?

CAROL. It's becoming drearypegs.

COLONEL. Quiet, Dumpling. Let me handle this.

BRINDSLEY. What's there to handle, sir?

COLONEL. If you think I'm going to let my daughter marry a born liar, you're very much mistaken.

HAROLD. Marry!

CAROL. Well, that's the idea.

HAROLD. You and this young lady, Brin?

CAROL. Are what's laughingly known as engaged. Subject of course to Daddy's approval.

HAROLD. Well! (*Amazed at the news, and at the fact that* BRINDSLEY *hasn't confided in him.*) What a surprise!

BRINDSLEY. We were keeping it a secret.

HAROLD. Evidently. How long's this been going on, then?

BRINDSLEY. A few months.

HAROLD. You old slyboots.

BRINDSLEY. (*Nervous.*) I hope you approve, Harold.

HAROLD. Well, I must say, you know how to keep things to yourself.

BRINDSLEY. (*Placatingly.*) I meant to tell you, Harold . . . I really did. You were the one person I was going to tell.

HAROLD. Well why didn't you, then?

BRINDSLEY. I don't know. I just never got around to it.

HAROLD. (*Huffy.*) Well, it's your business. There's no obligation to share confidences. I've only been your neighbour for three years. I've always assumed there was more than a geographical closeness between us, but I was obviously mistaken.

BRINDSLEY. Oh, don't start getting huffy, Harold.

HAROLD. I'm not getting anything. I'm just saying it's surprising, that's all. Surprising and somewhat disappointing.

BRINDSLEY. Oh look, Harold, please understand—

HAROLD. (*Shrill.*) There's no need to say anything! (*Into the* COLONEL's *face.*) It'll just teach me in future

not to bank too much on friendship. It's Silly Me again!
Silly, stupid, trusting me!

COLONEL. Good God!

(MISS FURNIVAL *rises in agitation and gropes her way
to the drinks table. She carries* HAROLD'S *travelling-
bag in mistake for her own and puts it down by the
table. Its weight makes her stoop.*)

CAROL. (*Wheedling.*) Oh come, Mr. Gorringe. We
haven't told anybody. Not one single soulipegs. Really.

COLONEL. At the moment, Dumpling, there's nothing
to tell. And I'm not sure there's going to be!

BRINDSLEY. Look, sir, we seem to have got off on the
wrong foot. If it's my fault, I apologize.

MISS FURNIVAL. (*Groping about on the drinks table.*)
My father always used to say, "To err is human: to forgive divine."

CAROL. I thought that was somebody else.

MISS FURNIVAL. (*Blithely.*) So many people copied
him. (*She finds the open bottle of gin, lifts it and sniffs
it.*)

CAROL. May I help you, Miss Furnival?

MISS FURNIVAL. No, thank you, Miss Melkett. I'm
just getting myself another bitter lemon. That is,—if I
may, Mr. Miller.

BRINDSLEY. Of course. Help yourself.

MISS FURNIVAL. Thank you, most kind! (*She pours
more gin into her glass and returns slowly to sit Upstage
on the edge of the rostrum.*)

COLONEL. Well sir, I'll overlook your damn peculiar
behaviour, but understand this, Miller. My daughter's
dear to me. You show me you can look after her, and
I'll consider the whole thing most favourably. I can't
say fairer than that, can I?

CAROL. Of course he can look after me, Daddy. His
works are going to be world-famous. In five years I'll
feel just like Mrs. Michaelangelo.

(MISS FURNIVAL *pauses in her cross.*)

HAROLD. (*Loftily.*) There wasn't a Mrs. Michaelangelo, actually.

CAROL. (*Irritated.*) Wasn't there?

HAROLD. No. He had passionate feelings of a rather different nature.

CAROL. Really, Mr. Gorringe. I didn't know that. (*She puts out her tongue at him.* MISS FURNIVAL *completes her cross and sits.*)

BRINDSLEY. Look, Harold, I'm sorry if I've hurt your feelings.

HAROLD. (*Loftily.*) You haven't.

BRINDSLEY. I know I have. Please forgive me.

CAROL. Oh, do, Mr. Gorringe. Quarrelling is so dreary. I hope we're all going to be great friends.

HAROLD. I'm not sure that I can contemplate a friendly relationship with a viper.

MISS FURNIVAL. Remember: to err is human, to forgive divine!

COLONEL. (*Irritated.*) You just said that, Madam.

(CLEA *enters, gaily dressed, and carrying an air-bag. She wears dark glasses. She advances boldly into the room, in silence; pauses; takes off the glasses—and finds no difference in the light.*)

MISS FURNIVAL. (*Downing her gin happily.*) Did I?

CAROL. Brin's not really a viper. He's just artistic, aren't you, darling?

BRINDSLEY. Yes, darling.

(CAROL *sends him an audible kiss across the astonished* CLEA. *He returns it, equally audibly.*)

CAROL. (*Winningly.*) Come on, Mr. Gorringe. It really is a case of forgive and forgettipegs.

HAROLD. Is it really pegs?

CAROL. Have another Ginette and lime. I'll have one with you. (*She rises and mixes the drink.*)

HAROLD. (*Rising.*) Oh, all right. I don't mind if I do.

CAROL. Let me mix it for you.

HAROLD. Ta. (*He crosses to her, putting his empty glass into* CLEA'S *hand.* CAROL *takes it out of her hand immediately.*) I must say there's nothing nicer than having a booze-up with a pretty girl.

CAROL. (*Archly.*) You haven't seen me yet.

HAROLD. Oh, I just know it. Brindsley always had wonderful taste. I've often said to him, you've got the same taste in ladies as I have in porcelain. (CAROL *puts the full glass into* CLEA'S *hand. She swallows it, hands the empty glass to* HAROLD, *and sidles quickly away towards the sofa.*) Ta.

(HAROLD *and* BRINDSLEY—*one from Upstage Left, and one from mid-stage Right—also move to the sofa.* ALL THREE, CLEA *in the middle, sit on it, on the word* "flattering," *and cross their legs in unison.*)

BRINDSLEY. Harold!

CAROL. Oh, don't be silly, Brin! Why be so modest? It's nothing to be ashamed about. If anything, it's rather flattering. I found a photograph of one of his bits from two years ago, and I must say she was pretty stunning— (CLEA *looks pleased.*) —in a blowsy sort of way. (CLEA *looks furious.*)

HAROLD. Which one was that, then? I suppose she means Clea.

CAROL. Did you know her, Mr. Gorringe?

HAROLD. Oh, yes. She's been around a long time.

(BRINDSLEY *nudges* CLEA *warningly—imagining she is* HAROLD. CLEA *gently bumps* HAROLD.)

CAROL. (*Surprised.*) Has she?

HAROLD. Oh yes, dear. Or am I speaking out of turn?

BRINDSLEY. Not at all. I've told Carol all about Clea. (*He bangs* CLEA *again, a little harder—who correspondingly bumps against* HAROLD.) Though I must say, Harold, I'm surprised you call three months "a long time."

(CLEA *shoots him a look of total outrage at this lie.* HAROLD *is also astonished.*)

CAROL. What was she like?

BRINDSLEY. (*Meaningfully, into* CLEA's *ear.*) I suppose you can hardly remember her, Harold.

HAROLD. (*Speaking across her.*) Why on earth shouldn't I?

BRINDSLEY. Well, since it was two years ago, you've probably forgotten.

HAROLD. Two years?!

BRINDSLEY. *Two years ago!* (*He punches* CLEA *so hard —that the rebound knocks* HAROLD *off the sofa, drink and all.*)

HAROLD. (*Rising and dusting himself off: spitefully.*) Well, now since you mention it, I remember her perfectly. I mean, she's not one you can easily forget!

CAROL. Was she pretty?

HAROLD. No, not at all. In fact, I'd say the opposite. Actually she was rather plain.

BRINDSLEY. She wasn't!

HAROLD. I'm just giving my opinion.

BRINDSLEY. You've never given it before.

HAROLD. (*Leaning over* CLEA.) I was never asked! But since it's come up, I always thought she was ugly. For one thing, she had teeth like a picket fence—yellow and spiky. And for another, she had bad skin.

BRINDSLEY. She had nothing of the kind!

HAROLD. She did. I remember it perfectly. It was like new pink wallpaper, with an old grey crumbly paper underneath.

MISS FURNIVAL. Quite right, Mr. Gorringe. I hardly ever saw her, but I do recall her skin. It was a strange colour, as you say—and very coarse . . . Not soft, as the skins of young ladies should be, if they *are* young ladies.

HAROLD. Aye, that's right. Coarse.

MISS FURNIVAL. And rather lumpy.

HAROLD. Very lumpy.

BRINDSLEY. (*Rising.*) This is disgraceful.

HAROLD. You knew I never liked her, Brindsley. She was too clever by half.

CAROL. You mean she was as pretentious as her name? (CLEA, *who has been reacting to this last exchange of comments about her like a spectator at a tennis match, now reacts to* CAROL *open-mouthed.*) I bet she was. That photograph I found showed her in a dirndl and a sort of sultry peasant blouse. She looked like "The Bartered Bride" done by Lloyds Bank.

(*They laugh,* BRINDSLEY *hardest of all.* CLEA *now rises and, guided by the noise, aims her hand and slaps his face.*)

BRINDSLEY. Ahh!

CAROL. What's wrong?

MISS FURNIVAL. What is it, Mr. Miller?

BRINDSLEY. (*Furious.*) That's not very funny, Harold. What the hell's the matter with you?

(CLEA *makes her escape.*)

HAROLD. (*Indignant.*) With me?

BRINDSLEY. Well, I'm sure it wasn't the Colonel.

COLONEL. What wasn't, sir?

(BRINDSLEY, *groping about, catches* CLEA *by the bottom, and instantly recognizes her.*)

BRINDSLEY. (*In horror.*) Clea!

(CLEA *breaks loose and moves away from him. During the following he tries to find her in the dark, and she narrowly avoids him.*)

COLONEL. What?

BRINDSLEY. I was just remembering her, sir. You're all talking the most awful nonsense. She was beautiful . . . And anyway, Harold, you just said I was famous for my taste in women.

HAROLD. Aye, but it had its lapses.

BRINDSLEY. (*Frantically moving about.*) Rubbish! She was beautiful and tender and considerate and kind and loyal and witty and adorable in every way!

CAROL. You told me she was as cozy as a steel razor blade.

BRINDSLEY. Did I? . . . Surely not. No. It doesn't sound like me!

(CLEA *reaches the table, picks up a bottle of vodka, and moves threateningly towards the deb from behind.*)

CAROL. You said to me in this room when I asked you what she was like, "She was a painter. Very honest. Very clever, and just about as cozy—"

BRINDSLEY. (*Marching towards her; exasperated.*) As a steel razor blade! Well then, I said it. So bloody what?

CAROL. So nothing!

(*She moves aside so that he bumps straight into* CLEA. *They instantly embrace,* CLEA *twining herself around him, her vodka bottle held aloft. A tiny pause.*)

COLONEL. If that boy isn't touched, I don't know the meaning of the word!

CAROL. What's all this talk about her being kind and tender, all of a sudden?

BRINDSLEY. (*Tenderly, holding* CLEA.) She could be. On occasion. Very.

CAROL. Very rare occasions, I imagine.

BRINDSLEY. Not so rare. Not so rare at all. (*He leads her softly past the irritated* CAROL, *towards the stairs.*)

CAROL. Meaning what, exactly? . . . Brindsley, I'm talking to you.

BRINDSLEY. (*Sotto voce, into* CLEA'S *ear as they stand just behind* HAROLD.) I can explain. Go up to the bedroom. Wait for me there.

HAROLD. (*In amazement: thinking he is being addressed.*) Now? Do you think this is quite the moment?

BRINDSLEY. Oh, God! . . . I wasn't talking to you.

CAROL. What did you say?

HAROLD. (*To* CAROL.) I think he wants *you* upstairs. (*Slyly.*) For what purpose, I can't imagine.

COLONEL. They're going to do some more of that plotting, I daresay.

MISS FURNIVAL. Lover's talk, Colonel.

COLONEL. Very touching, I'm sure.

(BRINDSLEY *pushes* CLEA *ahead of him up the stairs. She now has picked up* MISS FURNIVAL'S *bag from the sofa, leaving her own air-bag on it.*)

MISS FURNIVAL. "Journeys end in Lovers meeting," as my father always used to say.

COLONEL. What an original father you seem to have had, Madam.

(CAROL *joins the* OTHER TWO *on the stairs. We see* ALL THREE *groping blindly up to the bedroom,* BRINDSLEY'S *hands on* CLEA'S *hips,* CAROL'S *on* BRINDSLEY'S.)

CAROL. (*With a conspirator's stage whisper.*) What is it, darling? Has something gone wrong? What can't you move?

(*This next dialogue: Sotto Voce:*)

BRINDSLEY. Nothing. It's all back—every bit of it—Except the sofa, and I've covered that up.

CAROL. You mean, we can have lights?

BRINDSLEY. Yes . . . NO!

CAROL. Why not?

BRINDSLEY. Never mind!

CAROL. Why do you want me in the bedroom?

BRINDSLEY. I don't. Go away!

CAROL. Charming! (*She retreats Downstage and sits on the sofa next to* HAROLD.)

BRINDSLEY. I didn't mean that.

COLONEL. There you are. They are plotting again! What the hell is going on up there?

BRINDSLEY. I've just remembered—there may be a flashlight under my bed. I keep it to blind burglars with. Have another drink, Colonel! (*He goes into bedroom, pushing* CLEA *ahead of him and shuts the door.*)

COLONEL. What d'you mean, another? I haven't had one yet.

MISS FURNIVAL. (*Rising.*) Oh! Poor Colonel! Let me get you one.

COLONEL. I can get one for myself, thank you. Let me get you another lemonade.

MISS FURNIVAL. No thank you, Colonel, I'll manage myself. It's good practice!

(*They move across to the bar as in a slow motion race.*)

CLEA. (*On the bed.*) So this is what they mean by a blind date. What the hell is going on?

BRINDSLEY. Nothing! Only Georg Bamberger is coming to see my work tonight, and we've got a main fuse.

CLEA. Is that a reason for all this furtive clutching?

BRINDSLEY. Look, I can't explain things at the moment.

(CAROL'S *voice.*)

CLEA. Who's that frightful gel?

BRINDSLEY. Just a friend.

CLEA. She sounded more than that.

BRINDSLEY. Well if you must know, it's Carol. I've told you about her.

CLEA. The idiot deb?

BRINDSLEY. She's a very sweet girl. As a matter of fact we've become very good friends in the last six weeks.

CLEA. How good?

BRINDSLEY. Just good.

CLEA. And have you become friends with her father too?

BRINDSLEY. If it's any of your business, they just dropped in to meet Mr. Bamberger.

CLEA. What was it you wanted to tell me on the phone tonight?

BRINDSLEY. Nothing.

CLEA. You're lying!

BRINDSLEY. Ah, here comes the inquisition! Look, Clea, if you ever loved me, just slip away quietly with no more questions and I'll come 'round later and explain everything, I promise.

CLEA. I don't believe you.

BRINDSLEY. (*Getting on to the bed and kissing her.*) Please, darling . . . Please . . . please . . . *please!*

COLONEL. At last . . . a decent glass of Scotch. Are you getting your lemonade?

MISS FURNIVAL. (*Pouring out the gin.*) Oh yes, thank you, Colonel.

COLONEL. I'm just wonderin' if this Bamberger is goin' to show up at all. He's half an hour late already.

HAROLD. Oh! That's nothing, Colonel. Millionaires are always late. It's their thing.

MISS FURNIVAL. (*Weaving a little across the room, to sit on the dais.*) I'm sure, you're right, Mr. Gorringe. That's how I imagine them. Hands like silk, and always two hours late.

CAROL. Brin's been up there a long time. What can he be doing?

HAROLD. Maybe he's got that Clea hidden away in his bedroom, and they're having a tete a tete!

CAROL. What a fragrant suggestion, Mr. Gorringe.

BRINDSLEY. No one in the world kisses like you.

CLEA. I missed you so badly, Brin. I had to see you. I've thought about nothing else these past six weeks. Brin, I made the most awful mistake walking out.

BRINDSLEY. Clea—PLEASE!

CLEA. I mean we've known each other for four years. We can't just throw each other away like old newspapers.

BRINDSLEY. I don't see why not. You know my politics, you've heard my gossip, and you've certainly been through my entertainment section.

CLEA. Well, how about your Colour Supplement?

BRINDSLEY. Darling, can't you trust me just for an hour?

CLEA. Of course I can, darling. You don't want me down there?

BRINDSLEY. Right.

CLEA. Then I'll stay here. I'll get undressed and go quietly to bed. When you've got rid of them all, I'll be waiting.

BRINDSLEY. That's a terrible idea!

CLEA. I think it's lovely. (*Pulling him on to the bed.*) A little happy relaxation for us both.

BRINDSLEY. I'm perfectly relaxed!

CAROL. Brindsley!

CLEA. "Too solemn for day, too sweet for night. Come not in darkness come not in light." That's me, isn't it?

BRINDSLEY. Of course not. I just can't explain now, that's all.

CLEA. Oh, very well, you can explain later . . . in bed!

BRINDSLEY. Not tonight, Clea.

CLEA. Either that or I come down and discover your sordid secret.

BRINDSLEY. There is no sordid secret!

CLEA. Then you won't mind my coming down!

COLONEL and CAROL. BRINDSLEY!

BRINDSLEY. Oh God!! . . . All right, stay. Only keep quiet. Blackmailing bitch! (*Opening the door: very sweetly.*) Yes, my sweet?

CAROL. What are you doing up there? You've been an eternity!

BRINDSLEY. I'm just looking in the bathroom, my darling. You never know what you might find in that clever little cabinet!

COLONEL. Are you trying to madden me, sir? Are you trying to put me in a fury?

BRINDSLEY. Certainly not, sir!

COLONEL. I warn you, Miller, it's not difficult. In the old days in the regiment I was known for my furies . . . I was famous for my furies . . . do you hear?

CLEA. (*Singing.*) I may sing! . . . (*She goes off into the bathroom.*)

BRINDSLEY. (*Singing.*) I may knock your teeth in!

COLONEL. What did you say?

CAROL. BRIN! How dare you talk to Daddy like that!

BRINDSLEY. Oh! I—I—I wasn't talkin' to Daddy like that—

CAROL. Then who *were* you talking to?

BRINDSLEY. I was talking to no one! Myself I was talking to. I was saying, "If I keep groping about up here like this, I might knock my teeth in!"

COLONEL. Mad! Mad! Mad as the south wind! It's the only explanation—you've got yourself engaged to a lunatic.

CAROL. There's something going on up there, and I'm coming up to find out what it is. Do you hear me, Brin?

BRINDSLEY. CAROL!

CAROL. I'm not such a fool as you take me for. I know when you're hiding something. Your voice goes all deceitful—very foxipegs!

BRINDSLEY. Darling, please. That's not very ladylike! . . . I'm sure the Colonel won't approve of you entering a man's bedroom in the dark!

CAROL. (*Climbing the stairs.*) I'm comin' up, Brindsley, I'm comin' up!

BRINDSLEY. I'm comin' down. We'll all have a nice cozy drink—

SCHUPPANZIGH. (*Off.*) 'Allo please? Mr. Miller? Mr. Miller? I've come as was arranged.

(*They freeze.*)

BRINDSLEY. My God, it's Bamberger!
CAROL. Bamberger?
BRINDSLEY. Yes, Bamberger! (*He moves downstairs; she follows him.*)

(*Enter* SCHUPPANZIGH, *wearing a large coat of black oil-skin, labelled in huge white letters LONDON ELEC-TRICITY BOARD. He also a peaked cap, and bicycle clips, and carries a large workbag, similary labelled, and spilling over with wires. He gropes his way into the room, turning a gentle circle as he does so, so that the entire audience sees the legend on his back.*)

SCHUPPANZIGH. You must have thought I was never coming!
BRINDSLEY. Not at all. I'm delighted you could spare the time. I know how busy you are. I'm afraid we have had the most idiotic disaster. We've had a fuse.

(SCHUPPANZIGH *puts down his bag on the floor, fairly far Downstage, near the trap and takes off his coat.*)

HAROLD. (*To* BRINDSLEY.) You'll have to speak up, dear. He's stone deaf!
BRINDSLEY. (*Shouting.*) We've had a fuse! Not the best conditions for seeing sculpture.
SCHUPPANZIGH. Not to worry. Here—I have a torch!

(*He produces it from his bag, and shines it into their faces triumphantly. The Stage light, of course darkens immediately. All blink, and shield their faces.*)

CAROL. Oh, what a relief!

BRINDSLEY. How clever of you to carry a torch, sir. Or is it an essential part of the Connoisseur's equipment?

SCHUPPANZIGH. (*Bewildered.*) Connoisseur?

HAROLD. (*Whisper to* BRINDSLEY.) He's deaf! Speak up!

BRINDSLEY. Oh, yes! (*Yelling in* SCHUPPANZIGH'S *left ear.*) May I introduce Colonel Melkett!

(*All the guests line up to meet him, from Stage Right, shout their line into his right ear, as they shake his hand.*)

COLONEL. (*Roaring.*) A great honour, sir! (*Goes Upstage, Right.*)

(*The poor man flinches with the blast.*)

BRINDSLEY. Miss Carol Melkett!

CAROL. (*Screeching.*) Hallo, hallo! Terribly kind of you to take such an interest! (*Goes Upstage Right.*)

SCHUPPANZIGH. (*Recoiling.*) Not at all . . .

BRINDSLEY. (*Still yelling.*) A neighbour of mine—Harold Gorringe!

HAROLD. Very honoured, I'm sure! It's a real *thrill* meeting *you!* (*Crosses over, Left of* BRINDSLEY.)

SCHUPPANZIGH. (*Deafened.*) Oh! . . . (*He bangs his palm against his ear.*)

BRINDSLEY. And another neighbour: Miss Furnival!

(MISS FURNIVAL *comes forward and takes his hand.*)

MISS FURNIVAL. I'm afraid we've all been taking refuge from the *storm* as it were! (*Feeling his hands.*) Oh they are softer. Much, much softer! . . . (*She curtsies drunkenly.*)

BRINDSLEY. Miss Furnival,—*please!*

(HAROLD *reaches across and helps her to her feet, then leads her to the chair by the drinks table.*)

SCHUPPANZIGH. Excuse me, please, but why are you all shouting at me? I'm not deaf.

BRINDSLEY. (*To* HAROLD.) You told me he was.

HAROLD. I read he was.

MISS FURNIVAL. My father was.

BRINDSLEY. I'm terribly sorry, sir. A misunderstanding.

HAROLD. (*Fawningly.*) May I ask, sir, where you purchased that smart little cap?

SCHUPPANZIGH. My cap?

CAROL. Yes,—it's so chic! Wildly original!

SCHUPPANZIGH. But surely you've seen them before? We all have them.

HAROLD. You mean it's some kind of club. I bet it's very exclusive!

SCHUPPANZIGH. (*Giggling.*) Oh yes! Absolutely impossible to get into! . . . (*They all laugh.*)

MISS FURNIVAL. My father always used to say, it is easier for a rich man to go through the eye of a needle, than for a camel to enter heaven.

HAROLD. (*Sotto voce.*) Ferny!

SCHUPPANZIGH. (*Shining his torch at the sculpture.*) What an extraordinary object! May I look?

BRINDSLEY. Of course! Please! . . .

SCHUPPANZIGH. (*Examining it with fierce concentration.*) Fascinating!

BRINDSLEY. I like to think of that piece as representing the two needles of man's unrest. Self Love and Self Hate. They lead to the same point, do you see?

SCHUPPANZIGH. It's obvious.

HAROLD. It is?

SCHUPPANZIGH. They have the clarity of all great art.

COLONEL. Great art? You mean to say you like it?

SCHUPPANZIGH. Very much. Don't you?

COLONEL. Oh,—by all means, yes. Yes. Of course.

SCHUPPANZIGH. I hope you do. It is simple, but not

simple-minded. It is ingenious but not ingenuous. Above all it has real moral force. Of how many modern works can you say that, good people?

MISS FURNIVAL. (*Drunkenly.*) Oh none, really. None!

SCHUPPANZIGH. I hope I don't lecture. It is a fault with me.

CAROL. (*Gushing.*) Not at all. I could listen all night!

MISS FURNIVAL. It's so terribly profound . . .

COLONEL. I don't know anythin' about this myself, sir, but it's an honour to listen to you.

SCHUPPANZIGH. (*More and more extravagantly.*) Don't listen:—*look! Witness! Revere!* . . . Here—amazingly— I feel the passionate embrace of Similarities to create an orgasm of Opposites. Unprecedented, good people! Here— at last!—is incest in ironwork!

CAROL. Oh, how super!

MISS FURNIVAL. Jolly well done, Mr. Miller!

HAROLD. Well I never! Who'd have thought I'd been living next door to a genius!

SCHUPPANZIGH. You should charge immense sums for this. I hope it is very, very expensive.

BRINDSLEY. Er . . .

CAROL. But of course.

SCHUPPANZIGH. How much?

BRINDSLEY. Fifty—

CAROL. Five hundred guineas!

SCHUPPANZIGH. Ah, so. Very cheap. But then what is cheap or dear? There is no way possible to relate Beauty and Money. An equation in which one term is Reality and the other Unreality cannot be considered!

BRINDSLEY. Of course not.

CAROL. (*Briskly.*) Will you have it, then?

SCHUPPANZIGH. Me?

BRINDSLEY. Darling, aren't you rushing things a little! (*To* SCHUPPANZIGH.) Perhaps you would like to see my main work, in the studio.

SCHUPPANZIGH. Thank you, no. As Moses discovered,

it is sufficient to glimpse milk and honey. One does not have to wolf them down.

BRINDSLEY. Thank you. Well . . .

SCHUPPANZIGH. (*Beaming back.*) Well. . . .

BRINDSLEY. Well, well.

CAROL. Well?

COLONEL. Well?

HAROLD. Would you like it, then?

SCHUPPANZIGH. Very much.

MISS FURNIVAL. Oh, bravo, Mr. Miller! Bravo!

COLONEL. For five hundred guineas???

SCHUPPANZIGH. Certainly. If I had it.

(*General laughter.*)

HAROLD. According to the Sunday Mirror, you must be worth at least a hundred million pounds.

SCHUPPANZIGH. The Sunday papers are notoriously ill informed. According to my last bank statement, I was worth ninety six pounds, two shillings.

HAROLD. You mean, you've gone broke?

SCHUPPANZIGH. No, I mean I never had any more.

COLONEL. Now look, sir, I know millionaires are supposed to be eccentric, but this is gettin' tiresome.

CAROL. Daddy, shh!

SCHUPPANZIGH. Millionaires? But who do you think I am?

COLONEL. Dammit, man,—you must know who you are!

CAROL. Mr. Bamberger, is this some kind of joke you like to play?

SCHUPPANZIGH. Excuse me, that is not my name.

BRINDSLEY. It isn't?

SCHUPPANZIGH. Certainly not. My name is Schuppanzigh. Franz Immanuel Schuppanzigh. Born in Weimar 1905. Student of Philosophy at Heidelberg, 1934. Refugee to this country, 1938. Regular employment ever since with— (*Proudly clicking his heels.*) The LONDON ELECTRICITY BOARD!

CAROL. Electricity?

MISS FURNIVAL. (*Starting up.*) Electricity?

BRINDSLEY. You mean you're not?—

HAROLD. Of course he's not!

SCHUPPANZIGH. But who did you imagine I was?

HAROLD. (*Furious.*) How dare you? (*He snatches the electrician's torch.*)

SCHUPPANZIGH. (*Retreating.*) Please?—

HAROLD. (*Driving him off the dais and across the Stage.*) Of all the nerve, coming in here talking to us about orgasms and incest, and all the time you're just to mend the fuses!

COLONEL. I agree with you? sir! (*Snatching the torch from* HAROLD *and shining it pitilessly into* SCHUPPANZIGH'S *face.*) It's monstrous!

SCHUPPANZIGH. (*Bewildered.*) It is?

COLONEL. You come in here (*Raising his voice.*) *pretending to be deaf!*—and proceed to harangue your employers, unasked and uninvited!

SCHUPPANZIGH. Excuse me, but I *was* invited!

COLONEL. Don't answer back. Miller, show this feller to his work! (*He thrusts the torch into* SCHUPPANZIGH'S *hand.*)

BRINDSLEY. The mains are in the cellar. Do you mind?

SCHUPPANZIGH. (*Exasperated.*) Why should I mind? It's why I came here after all!

BRINDSLEY. One would never know it!

SCHUPPANZIGH. (*Flashing the torch on the sofa; instantly enchanted.*) Ahh! Now there is a really beautiful piece of furniture!

BRINDSLEY. (*Flinging himself on to the sofa.*) Why don't you just go into the cellar?! (*He lies all over the sofa in a desperate set of poses, attempting to cover it with his body.*)

SCHUPPANZIGH. (*Exasperated too.*) All right!! Where is it?

BRINDSLEY. Darling, open the trapdoor please!

CAROL. Me?

COLONEL. Well that's very gallant of you, Miller!

CAROL. (*Peeved.*) It certainly is!

BRINDSLEY. (*Writhing on the sofa.*) Lumbago, lumbago, lumbago! It often afflicts me after long spells in the dark. (*To* CAROL, *through gritted teeth.*) The *sofa!* . . .

CAROL. (*Understanding.*) Oh—yes! . . . (*Gushing.*) Oh, has it come back? You poor *darling!* Just you lie there—don't make a single little move! I'll do everything! (*Kiss noise.*) Mmm!

BRINDSLEY. (*Kiss noise.*) Mmm!

HAROLD. (*Going to the trap.*) Never mind. I'll do it. I'm not so frail as our wilting friend. (*Tugging open the trap door: To* SCHUPPANZIGH.) Come on, down you go, you! (*As* SCHUPPANZIGH *gathers up his bag and coat, and drops them through the trap.*) Come on, get a move on!

SCHUPPANZIGH. All right! (*Entering the trap.*) So: farewell. I leave the light of Art for the dark of Science!

HAROLD. Let's have a little less of your lip, shall we?

SCHUPPANZIGH. Excuse me.

(*He descends the trap, taking the torch with him, and* HAROLD *slams the door down on top of him. Instant light, of course, on Stage: all react to the flood of "darkness" again—except* BRINDSLEY *who leaps backwards off the sofa and moves swiftly to the studio curtains, which he gingerly draws open. At the same moment* MISS FURNIVAL *sits on the sofa.*)

COLONEL. Incredible! Absolutely incredible! In the old days people like that would have been fired on the spot for impertinence.

(MISS FURNIVAL *collapses her length on the sofa.*)

CAROL. Daddy's absolutely right. Ever since the Beatles the lower classes think they can behave exactly as they like. (BRINDSLEY *stealthily pulls the sofa into the studio, bearing in it the supine* MISS FURNIVAL, *who waves good-bye to the company with the vague grandeur of a first-class passenger departing on an ocean liner.*) And Miss Furnival was only saying before you came, daddy, nowadays England's entirely in the hands of foreigners. Weren't you, Miss Furnival?

(*The curtains close on her. The* COLONEL *starts groping his way Upstage to find the sofa and sit on it. During the following* BRINDSLEY *returns, pauses a second, realises he has to put something in place of the missing sofa, moves to where the decorated boxes stand on top of each other Upstage Right by the door, takes off the top one, and puts it down just as the travelling* COLONEL *touches it, mistakes it for the sofa, and makes to sit.* BRINDSLEY, *not satisfied with the position, moves it further over Stage Right, on his knees: the* COLONEL *sits on nothing—and almost falls. He moves to his Right; touches the box, and again makes to sit. Again* BRINDSLEY *moves the box, and again the* COLONEL *almost falls backwards.* BRINDSLEY *moves the box a third time, but this time the* COLONEL *sits down so quickly he traps* BRINDSLEY'S *hand beneath his weight.*)

COLONEL. Of course it is. Has been for years! That's what we fought the war for, dumpling—to fill the place with a lot of peole like that. Marvelous! Fight their war for 'em! bankrupt yerself! make yerself a beggar nation throughout the civilised world,—laughin' stock everywhere—and what for? (*First false sit.*) People like that! Bounders! Bolshie bounders! (*Second false sit.*) Ungrateful, insubordinate shower of Krauts! (*Final sit, trapping* BRINDSLEY.) Of course all this seems very square to you no doubt, Miller, eh? Very middle class and stuffy, what? . . .

(BRINDSLEY *is desperately trying to free himself. Suddenly from close behind them* MISS FURNIVAL *starts singing "Rock of Ages" in a high drunken voice. The* COLONEL *rises slowly in alarm—freeing* BRINDSLEY, *who falls onto the floor, Mid-stage, Right.* CAROL *and* HAROLD *freeze with astonishment. As she reaches the third phrase "Let my tears flow evermore."* CLEA *comes in above from the bathroom, Stage Left, wearing the top half of* BRINDSLEY'S *pyjamas, and nothing else. She carries her vodka bottle. Attracted by the singing she moves across the bedroom to the door.)*

BRINDSLEY. None of this evening is happening.

CAROL. Cheer up, darling. In a few minutes everything will be all right. Mr. Bamberger will arrive in the light—he'll adore your work, and give you twenty thousand pounds for your whole collection.

(CLEA *opens the door at the top of the stairs.*)

BRINDSLEY. (*Sarcastic.*) Oh, yes!

CAROL. Then we can buy a super Georgian house and live what's laughingly known as happily ever after. I want to leave this place just as soon as we're married.

(CLEA *hears this. Her mouth opens wide.*)

BRINDSLEY. (*Nervously.*) Sssh!

CAROL. Why? I don't want to live in a slum for our first couple of years—like other newlyweds.

BRINDSLEY. Sssh! Ssssh!

CAROL. What's the matter with you?

BRINDSLEY. The gods listen, darling. They've given me a terrible night so far. They may do worse.

CAROL. (*Cooing.*) I know, darling. You've had a filthy evening. Poor babykins. But I'll fight them with you. I don't care a fig for those naughty old Goddipegs. (*Look-*

*ing up.*) Do you hear? Not a single little fig! (CLEA *aims at the voice and sends a jet of vodka splashing over* CAROL.) *Ahh!*

BRINDSLEY. What is it?

CAROL. It's raining!

BRINDSLEY. Don't be stupid.

CAROL. I'm all wet!

BRINDSLEY. How can you be?

(CLEA *throws vodka over a wider area.* HAROLD *shrieks as it falls over him.*)

HAROLD. Hey, what's going on?

COLONEL. What the devil's the matter with you all? What are you hollerin' for? (*He gets a slug of vodka in the face.*) Ahh!! I'm drenched!

BRINDSLEY. (*Inspired.*) It's a leak—the water mains must have gone now.

(CLEA *raps the bottle gently on the stairs. There is a terrified silence.* ALL *look up.*)

HAROLD. Don't say there's someone else here.

BRINDSLEY. Good Lord!

COLONEL. Who's there? (*Silence from above.*) Come on! I know you're there!

BRINDSLEY. (*Improvising wildly.*) I bet you it's Mrs. Punnet.

(CLEA *looks astonished.*)

COLONEL. Who?

BRINDSLEY. (*For* CLEA'S *benefit.*) Mrs. Punnet. My cleaning woman. She does for me on Mondays, Wednesdays and Fridays.

CAROL. But its Sunday.

CAROL. Well, what would she be doing here now?

BRINDSLEY. I've just remembered—she rang up and said she'd look in about six to tidy up the place.

COLONEL. Dammit, man, it's almost eleven.

HAROLD. She's not that conscientious. She couldn't be!

COLONEL. Well, we'll soon see. (*Calling up.*) Mrs. Punnet?

BRINDSLEY. (*Desperately.*) Don't interrupt her. Leave her alone, sir . . . She doesn't like to be disturbed when she's working. Why don't we just leave her to potter around upstairs with her duster?

COLONEL. Let's first see if it's her. Mrs. Punnet, is that you? . . . *Mrs. Punnet!!*

(*A pause.*)

CLEA. (*Deciding on a cockney voice of great antiquity.*) Allo? Yes?

BRINDSLEY. It is! . . . Good heavens, Mrs. Punnet— what on earth are you doing up there?

CLEA. I'm just giving your bedroom a bit of a tidy, sir.

BRINDSLEY. At this time of night?

CLEA. (*The mischief in her begins to take over.*) Better late than never, sir as they say. I know how you like your bedroom to be nice and inviting when you're giving one of your parties.

BRINDSLEY. Yes, yes, yes, of course . . .

COLONEL. When did you come, madam?

CLEA. Just a few minutes ago, sir. I didn't like to disturb you, so I come on up 'ere.

HAROLD. Was it you pouring all that water on us, then?

CLEA. Water? Good 'eavens, I must have upset something. It's as black as Newgate's Knocker up 'ere. Are you playing one of your kinky games, Mr. Miller? (*She starts to come down the stairs.*)

BRINDSLEY. (*Distinctly.*) It is a fuse, Mrs. Punnet. The man's mending it now. The lights will be on any minute.

CLEA. Well, that'll be a relief for you, won't it? (*She dashes the vodka accurately into his face, passes him by and comes into the room.*)

BRINDSLEY. Yes, of course. Now why don't you just go on home?

CLEA. I'm sorry I couldn't come before, sir. I was delayed, you see. My Rosie's been taken queer again.

BRINDSLEY. I quite understand! (*He gropes around trying to hide her, but she continuously evades him.*)

CLEA. (*Relentlessly.*) It's her tummy. There's a lump under her belly button the size of a grapefruit.

HAROLD. Oh, how nasty!

CLEA. Horrid. Poor little Rosie. I said to her this evening, I said, "There's no good your being mulish, my girl. You're going to the hospital first thing tomorrow morning and getting yourself ultra-violated!"

BRINDSLEY. Well, hadn't you better be getting back to poor little Rosie? She must need you, surely?—And there's really nothing you can do here tonight.

CLEA. (*Meaningfully.*) Are you sure of that, sir?

BRINDSLEY. Positive, thank you.

(*She sits on the table. He approaches her from behind.*)

CLEA. I mean, I know what this place can be like after one of your evenings. A gypsy caravan isn't in it! Gin bottles all over the floor! Bras and panties in the sink! And God knows what—

(BRINDSLEY *muzzles her with his hand. She bites it hard and he drops to his knees in silent agony.*)

COLONEL. Please watch what you say, madam. You don't know it, but you're in the presence of Mr. Miller's fiancee.

CLEA. Fiancee?

COLONEL. Yes, and I am her father.

CLEA. Oh, Mr. Miller! I'm so 'appy for you! . . . Fiancee! Oh, sir! And you never told me!

BRINDSLEY. I was keeping it a surprise.

CLEA. Well, I never! Oh, how lovely! . . . May I kiss you sir, please?

BRINDSLEY. (*On his knees.*) Well yes, yes, of course . . .

(CLEA *finds his ear and twists it relentlessly.*)

CLEA. Oh, sir, I'm so pleased for you! And for *you,*
Miss, too!
CAROL. Thank you.
CLEA. (*To* COLONEL.) And for *you,* sir.
COLONEL. Thank you.
CLEA. (*Wickedly.*) You must be Miss Clea's father.
COLONEL. Miss Clea? I don't understand.

(*Triumphantly she sticks out her tongue at* BRINDSLEY,
*who collapses his length on the floor, face down, in
a gesture of total surrender. For him it is the end.
The evening can hold no further disasters for him.*)

CLEA. (*To* CAROL.) Well, I never! So you've got him
at last! Well done, Miss Clea! I never thought you would
—not after four years . . .
BRINDSLEY. No—no—no—no!
CLEA. Forgive me, sir, if I'm speaking out of turn, but
you must admit four years is a long time to be courting
one woman. Four days is stretching it a bit nowadays!
BRINDSLEY. (*Weakly.*) Mrs. Punnet, *please!*
CAROL. Four years!
CLEA. Well, yes, dear. It's been all of that and a bit
more really, hasn't it? (*In a stage whisper.*) And of
course it's just in time. It was getting a bit prominent,
your little bun in the oven. (CAROL *screeches with dis-
gust.* BRINDSLEY *covers his ears.*) Oh, Miss, I don't mean
that's why he popped the question. Of course it's not.
He's always been stuck on you. He told me so, not one
week ago, in this room. (*Sentimentally.*) "Mrs. Punnet,"
he says, "Mrs. Punnet, as far as I'm concerned you can
keep the rest of them—Miss Clea will always be on top
of the heap for me." "Oh," I says, "then what about that
debutante bit, Carol, the one you're always telling me

about?" "Oh, 'er," he says, "she's just a bit of Knightsbridge candyfloss. A couple of licks and you've 'ad 'er."

BRINDSLEY. *Ahhhhh!*

(*There is a long pause.* CLEA *is now sitting on the table, swinging her vodka bottle in absolute command of the situation.*)

COLONEL. (*Faintly; at last grappling with the situation.*) Did you say four years, madam?

CLEA. (*In her own voice. Quiet.*) Yes, Colonel. Four years, in this room.

HAROLD. I know that voice. It's Clea!

MISS FURNIVAL. (*Surprised.*) Clea!

CAROL. (*Horrified.*) Clea!

BRINDSLEY. (*Unconvincingly surprised.*) Clea!

CLEA. Surprised, Brin?

CAROL. (*Understanding.*) Clea!

COLONEL. I don't understand anything that's going on in this room.

CLEA. I know. It is a very odd room, isn't it? It's like a magic dark room, where everything happens the wrong way round. Rain falls indoors, the Daily comes at night and turns in a second from a nice maid into,—a nasty mistress.

BRINDSLEY. Be quiet, Clea!

CLEA. At last! One real word of protest! Have you finished lying, then? Have you eaten the last crumb of humble pie? Oh, you coward, you bloody coward! Just because you didn't want to marry me, did you have to settle for this lot?

CAROL. Marry! ·

COLONEL. Marry?

CLEA. Four years of meaning to end in this triviality! Miss Laughingly Known As and her Daddipegs!

CAROL. Stop her! She's disgusting.

COLONEL. How can I, for God's sake?

CAROL. (*Moving Downstage to above the rocking*

*chair.*) Well, where's all that bloody resource you keep talking about?!

(*The* COLONEL *goes to her but takes* CLEA's *hand by mistake.*)

COLONEL. Now calm down, Dumpling. Keep your head . . . There—hold my hand, that's it, now Daddy's here. Everything is under control. All right?

CLEA. (*Whispering.*) Are you sure that is your daughter's hand you're holding, Colonel?

COLONEL. What? Carol, isn't this your hand?

CAROL. No.

CLEA. You must have lived with your daughter for well over twenty years, Colonel. What remarkable use you've made of your eyes. (*There is another pause. The* COLONEL *moves away in embarrassment. Wickedly.*) All right! Kinky game time! Let's all play Guess the Hand.

(ALL *react, and try to move away.*)

HAROLD. Good God!

CLEA. Or would you rather play Guess the Lips, Harold?

CAROL. How disgusting!

CLEA. Well that's me, dear. I'm Queen Disgustipegs! Who's this? (*She seizes* CAROL's *hand and puts it into* HAROLD's.)

CAROL. I don't know.

CLEA. Guess.

CAROL. I don't know and I don't care.

CLEA. Oh, (*Mimicking* CAROL's *voice.*) go on. Have a go!

CAROL. It's Brin, of course: You can't trick me like that! It's Brindsley's stupid hand.

HAROLD. I'm afraid you're wrong. It's me.

CAROL. (*Struggling.*) It's not. You're lying.

HAROLD. (*Holding on.*) I'm not. I don't lie.

CAROL. You're lying! . . . You're lying!
HAROLD. I'm not. I don't lie!

(CAROL *breaks away and blunders Upstage. She is becoming hysterical.*)

CLEA. You try it, Harold. Take the hand on your right.
HAROLD. I'm not playing. It's a bloody silly game.
CLEA. Go on . . . (*She seizes his hand and puts it into* BRINDSLEY'S.) Well?
HAROLD. It's Brin.
BRINDSLEY. Yes.
CLEA. Well done!
CAROL. How does he know that? How does he know your hand and I don't?
BRINDSLEY. Calm down, Carol.
CAROL. Answer me! I want to know!
BRINDSLEY. Stop it!
CAROL. I won't!
BRINDSLEY. You're getting hysterical!
CAROL. Leave me alone! I want to go home!
MISS FURNIVAL. (*Off: in the studio.*) Prams! (*She staggers out, carrying* CLEA'S *air-bag. She speaks quickly, haughtily, in a flood of drunken outrage and resentment. All freeze.*) Prams! Prams in the Supermarket! All those hideous wire prams, full of babies and bottles! Cornflakes over there is all they say, and then they leave you to yourself! Biscuits over there! (*Pointing in different directions, like a mad signpost.*) cat food over there! fishcakes over there! Airwick over there! Pink stamps, green stamps, television dinners, pay as you go out,—oh daddy it's awful! . . . And then the Godless ones, Heathens in their leather jackets, laughing me to scorn! But not for long, oh no! Who shall stand when He appeareth? He'll strike them from their motorcycles! He'll dash their helmets to the ground. Yea, verily, I say unto thee— There shall be an end to gasoline! An end to petroleloleum! An end to cigarette puffing and jostling with hips.

Keep off! . . . Keep off! . . . Keep off! . . . It's shameful! . . . Off! . . . Off! . . . Offf! . . . (*She strikes out with the air-bag, moving rapidly across the Stage until she collides with* HAROLD. *He steadies her.*)

HAROLD. (*Gently.*) Come on, Ferny. I think it's time we went home.

MISS FURNIVAL. (*Pulling herself together.*) Yes. You're quite right. (*With an attempt at grandeur.*) I'm sorry, Mr. Miller, I can't wait any longer. Your millionaire is unpardonably late. Express my regrets, if you please. (*Leaning on* HAROLD, *she leaves, grandly. He shuts the door.*)

COLONEL. (*Grimly.*) You can express my regrets too, Miller, d'ye hear me? Mine too.

CAROL. And mine, Brindsley. You can express mine!

COLONEL. Come, dumpling. We're leavin'.

CAROL. Just one moment, daddy. Brindsley—

BRINDSLEY. What?

CAROL. Here. (*She takes off her engagement ring.*)

BRINDSLEY. What?

CAROL. Your ring. Take the bloody thing back! (*She throws it, and it hits the* COLONEL *in the eye.* BRINDSLEY *has ducked and is sitting on the table next to* CLEA.)

COLONEL. My eye! My damned eye! (CLEA *starts to laugh.*) Oh very droll, madam. Very droll indeed! (BRINDSLEY *begins to laugh too. They hold each other.* COLONEL *very quietly: with a mad, sinister colour to his voice.*) Miller. (*He advances Right to Left, above the table. Their laughter stops.*) Do you know what would have happend to a young lout in my day, who dared to treat a gel the way you have treated my Dumpling?

BRINDSLEY. Happened, sir?

COLONEL. (*Correcting his direction from* BRINDSLEY'S *voice.*) You would have been thrashed, sir.

BRINDSLEY. (*Rising simultaneously with* CLEA. *Like Babes in the Wood, clutching each other, they creep away Downstage Right.*) Thrashed, sir?

COLONEL. (*Following, slowly.*) You'd have felt the

mark of a father's horsewhip across your seducer's shoulders! (*During the next speech,* BRINDSLEY *and* CLEA, *tightly clasped together, do a soft impertinent tango together as they dance Upstage towards the door.*) You would have cried! You would have wept! You would have gone down on your cad's bended knees and begged my daughter's pardon for the insults you have offered her tonight! You'd have raised your guttersnipe voice in a piteous *scream* for mercy and forgiveness!—

(*A terrible scream is heard outside the door, coming from* HAROLD'S *flat and approaching nearer and nearer. In alarm the two dancers freeze—then break:* CLEA *to sit Downstage to near the trapdoor,* BRINDSLEY *backing a little away nervously on the diagonal Downstage Right. The door opens and* HAROLD, *wild-eyed with rage, and holding a lit taper, plunges into the room.*)

HAROLD. (*Finishing the scream.*) Ooooh! You—*villain!!*

BRINDSLEY. Harold—

HAROLD. You skunky, conniving little villain!

BRINDSLEY. (*Retreating before him.*) What's the matter?

HAROLD. (*Raging.*) Have you seen the state of my room? My room? My lovely room, the most elegant and cared for in this entire district—one chair turned absolutely upside down, one chair on top of another like a Portobello junkshop! And that's not all, is it, Brindsley? Oh no, that's not the worst by a long chalk, is it, Brindsley?

BRINDSLEY. (*Falling into the rocking chair.*) Long chalk?

HAROLD. Don't play the innocent with me. I thought I had a friend living all these years. I didn't know I was living opposite a Light-fingered Lenny!

BRINDSLEY. Harold!—

HAROLD. (*Hysterical.*) This is my reward, isn't it?—After years of looking after you, sweeping and tidying up this place, because you're too much of a slut to do it for yourself?—to have my best pieces stolen from me to impress your new girl friend and her daddy. Or did she help you?

BRINDSLEY. Harold, it was an emergency.

HAROLD. Don't talk to me: I don't want to know! I know what you think of me now . . . "Don't tell Harold about the engagement. He's not to be trusted. He's not a friend. He's just someone to steal things from!"

BRINDSLEY. You know that's not true.

HAROLD. (*Shrieking—in one hysterical breath.*) I know I was the last one to know—that's what I know! I have to find it out in a room full of strangers. Me, who's listened to more of your miseries in the small hours of the morning than anyone else would put up with! All your boring talk about women, hour after hour, as if no one's got troubles but you!

CLEA. She's getting hysterical, dear. Ignore her.

HAROLD. It's you who's going to be ignored, Clea! (*To* BRINDSLEY.) And as for you, all I can say about your engagement is this: you deserve each other, you and that little nit. (CAROL *gives a shriek.*) Oh, so you're there, are you?—Skulking in the shadows!

BRINDSLEY. Leave her alone!

HAROLD. I'm not going to touch her. I wouldn't demean myself! I just want my things and I'll be off! . . . Did you hear me, Brindsley? You give me my things now, or I'll call the police!

BRINDSLEY. Don't be ridiculous!

HAROLD. Item: one exquisite table lamp in white opaline, embossed with a garland of matchless ormolu.

BRINDSLEY. In the waste-paper basket.

HAROLD. My ears are deceiving me. Item: one irreplaceable Regency sofa, supported by claw legs and upholstered in a rich silk of deep bottle green.

BRINDSLEY. In the studio.

HAROLD. Unbelievable. Item: one Coalport vase, dated 1809, decorated on the rim with a pleasing design of daisies and peonies.

BRINDSLEY. On the floor.

HAROLD. On the floor. (*Picking it up, from under the chair, Upstage Left.*) You've even taken the flowers! . . . I'll come back for the lamp and sofa in a minute. (*Drawing himself up with all the offended dignity of which a* HAROLD GORRINGE *is capable.*) This is the end of our relationship, Brindsley. We won't be speaking again, I don't think. (*He twitches his raincoat off the table. Inside it, of course, is the Buddha, which rises high in the air and falls on the floor, or table, smashing beyond repair. There is a terrible silence. Slowly* HAROLD *scrutinises the wreckage. When at last he speaks, it is in the quiet voice of the very dangerous.*) I think I'm going to have to smash you, Brindsley.

BRINDSLEY. Now steady on, Harold.

HAROLD. (*Moving across the room, and thrusting the vase of flowers brutally into* CAROL'S *hands as he crosses.*) Yes, I'm very much afraid I'm going to have to smash you. . . . Smash for smash—that's fair do's. (*He pulls one of the long metal prongs out of the sculpture.*) Smash for smash. Smash for *smash!* (*He whirls the prong round his head, the taper still burning in his other hand.*)

BRINDSLEY. Stop it, Harold. You've gone mad!

COLONEL. Well done, sir. I think it's time for the reckoning! (*The* COLONEL *grabs the other prong and together they advance on* BRINDSLEY.)

BRINDSLEY. (*Retreating before them both.*) Now just a minute, Colonel. Be reasonable . . . Let's not revert to savages . . . Harold—I appeal to you! You've always had civilized instincts! Don't join the Army! . . .

CAROL. (*Tearing the flowers out of the vase and throwing them up in the air—then inverting the vase for a weapon. Her voice low, grim, as she stalks him.*) Get him, daddy. Get him. Get him. Get him! . . .

BRINDSLEY. *Clea!* Help!

(CLEA *leaps up and blows out the taper. LIGHTS ON FULL.*)

COLONEL. Dammit! . . . (BRINDSLEY *passes him. Patting his bottom.*) Careful, my little Dumpling. Keep out of the way.

HAROLD. (*To* CAROL.) Hush up, Colonel. We'll be able to hear him breathing.

COLONEL. Clever idea! Smart tactics, sir!

(*Silence. They listen.* BRINDSLEY *climbs carefully onto the table and silently pulls* CLEA *up after him.* HAROLD *and the* COLONEL, *prodding and slashing the darkness with their swords, grimly hunt their quarry. Twenty seconds. Suddenly, with a bang* SCHUPPANZIGH *opens the trap from below.* BOTH MEN *advance on it warily. The* ELECTRICIAN *disappears again below. They have almost reached it, on tip-toe, when there is another CRASH—this time from the hall. Someone has again tripped over the milk bottles.* HAROLD *and the* COLONEL *immediately swing round and start stalking Upstage, still on tip-toe. Enter* GEORG BAMBERGER. *He is quite evidently a millionaire. Dressed in the Gulbenkian manner, he wears a beard, an eye-glass, a frock-coat, a top-hat and an orchid. He carries a large deaf-aid. Bewildered, he advances into the room. Stealthily, the* TWO ARMED MEN *stalk him Upstage as he silently gropes his way Downstage and passes between them.*)

BAMBERGER. (*Speaking in a middle-aged German voice, as near to the voice of* SCHUPPANZIGH *as possible.*) Hallo, please! Mr. Miller?

(HAROLD *and the* COLONEL *spin round in a third direction.*)

HAROLD. Oh, it's the electrician!

BAMBERGER. Hallo, please?

COLONEL. What the devil are you doing up here? (SCHUPPANZIGH *appears at the trap.*) Have you mended the fuse?

HAROLD. Or are you going to keep us in the dark all night?

SCHUPPANZIGH. Don't worry. The fuse is mended. (*He comes out of the trap.*)

(BAMBERGER *goes round the Stage, Right.*)

HAROLD. Thank God for that.

BAMBERGER. (*Still groping around.*) Hallo, please? Mr. Miller—vere are you? Vy zis darkness? Is a joke, yes?

SCHUPPANZIGH. (*Incensed.*) Ah, no! That is not very funny, good people—just because I am a foreigner, to imitate my voice.

BAMBERGER. (*Imperiously.*) Mr. Miller! I have come to give attention to your sculptures!

SCHUPPANZIGH. Gott in himmel!

BAMBERGER. Gott in himmel!

BRINDSLEY. God, it's him! Bamberger!

CLEA. He's come!

HAROLD. Bamberger!

COLONEL. Bamberger!

(*They freeze. The* MILLIONAIRE *sets off, left, towards the open trap.*)

BRINDSLEY. Don't worry, Mr. Bamberger. We've had a fuse, but it's mended now.

BAMBERGER. (*Irritably.*) Mr. Miller!

CLEA. You'll have to speak up, darling. He's deaf.

BRINDSLEY. (*Shouting.*) Don't worry, Mr. Bamberger! We've had a fuse, but it's all right now! (*Standing on the table, he clasps* CLEA *happily.* BAMBERGER *steps over the open trap.*) Oh, Clea, that's true. Everything's all right now! Just in the nick of time!

(*But as he says this* BAMBERGER *turns and falls into the open trap door.* SCHUPPANZIGH *slams it to with his foot.*)

SCHUPPANZIGH. So! Here's now an end to your troubles! Like Jehovah in the Sacred Testament, I give you the most miraculous gift of the Creation! Light!
CLEA. Light!
BRINDSLEY. Oh, thank God. *Thank God!*

(SCHUPPANZIGH *gropes his way up to the switch.*)

HAROLD. (*Grimly.*) I wouldn't thank Him too soon, Brindsley, if I were you!
COLONEL. Nor would I, Brindsley, if I were you!
CAROL. Nor I, Brinny-winny, if I were you!
SCHUPPANZIGH. (*Grandly.*) Then thank *me!* For I shall play God for this second. (*Clapping his hands.*) Attend, all of you. God said: "Let there be light!" (*During these last phrases* HAROLD, CAROL *and the* COLONEL *slowly raise their weapons for the final assault on* BRINDSLEY.) And there was, good people, suddenly!—astoundingly!—instantaneously! — inconceivably — inexhaustibly — inextinguishably and eternally—LIGHT!

(SCHUPPANZIGH, *with a great flourish, flicks the LIGHT. Instant darkness. The turntable of the gramophone begins moving, and with a great crescendo wheeze the Sousa MARCH starts up again and blazes away in the blackness.*)

*END*

# APPENDIX

Here is an alternative set of scenes—and especially a Finale—to be used when there is no trap-door available.

This alternative is less funny—since nothing can really equal the effect of Bamberger's fall down the trap—and is only to be employed where it is genuinely impossible to use, or make a trap-door. Please use every effort, however, not to resort to the version appended here!

PETER SHAFFER

## A.

In the first scene with Miss Furnival, when Carol asks where the main switch of the house is to be found, Brindsley must reply, instead of "It's in the cellar"— "It's in the Studio. It's all sealed up. No one is allowed to touch it, except the electricity people."

## B.

At the end of the first scene with Schuppanzigh, when he is ordered down the trap, the new text should read:

BRINDSLEY. The mains are in the studio. Through there. Now do you mind?

SCHUPPANZIGH. Why should I mind? It's why I came here, after all!

BRINDSLEY. One would never know it!

SCHUPPANZIGH. (*Flashing the torch on the sofa: instantly enchanted.*) Ahh! Now there is a really beautiful piece of furniture!

BRINDSLEY. (*Flinging himself on the sofa.*) Why don't you just go into the studio? . . . (*Writhing on the sofa.*) Darling—please—show him the way, will you?

CAROL. Me?

COLONEL. Well, that's very gallant of you, Miller.

BRINDSLEY. Lumbago! Lumbago! Lumbago! It often afflicts me after long spells in the dark! . . . (*Through gritted teeth, to* CAROL.) The sofa! . . .

CAROL. Oh, yes! . . . (*Gushing.*) Has it come back?
You poor *darling!* Just lie there—don't make a single
little move. (*Taking the torch from* SCHUPPANZIGH.)
Now come along, pull yourself together!

SCHUPPANZIGH. (*Gathering up his bag.*) All right! I'm
coming.

CAROL. Well get a move on. We're all bored to death
with this dreary darkness.

SCHUPPANZIGH. (*To the company.*) So: farewell. I
leave the light of art for the dark of Science!

HAROLD. Let's have a little less of your lip, shall we?

SCHUPPANZIGH. Excuse me.

CAROL. This way.

(*She shows him into the studio through the curtains. The
light brighten. Instantly* BRINDSLEY *leaps off the
sofa and moves quickly to the door to see that it is
open. Then returns as quickly to try and pull it
across the room and through the door. A beat after
he gets up* MISS FURNIVAL *sits down on it; and as
he returns from the door, she lies her length upon
it. Stretching out one hand before him to feel if there
are obstacles, he pulls the sofa towards the door,
bearing on it a supine* MISS FURNIVAL, *waving cheer-
fully. Unfortunately the sofa will not fit through the
door. Hastily he pushes it backwards to its former
position.* MISS FURNIVAL *is quite giddy. During this,
the following dialogue:*)

HAROLD. Bloody cheek! The people you meet these
days. Honestly!

COLONEL. I quite agree with you, sir. In the old days
a feller like that would have been fired on the spot for
impertinence.

(MISS FURNIVAL *collapses her length on the sofa.*)

CAROL. Daddy's absolutely right. Ever since the

Beatles the Lower Classes think they can behave exactly as they like. And Miss Furnival was only saying before you came in, daddy: nowadays England is entirely in the hand of foreigners. Weren't you, Miss Furnival?

COLONEL. Of course it is! Has been for years! It's what we fought the war for, didn't yer know?—to fill the place with a lot of people like that. Marvellous! Fight their war for 'em. Make yerself a beggar nation throughout the civilised world—laughin' stock everywhere—and what for? People like that! Bounders! Bolshie bounders! (*In a panic* BRINDSLEY *realises he can't take the sofa into the studio—reaches into the top box of the pile near the door and pulls out a large blanket, which he drops over the whole sofa,* MISS FURNIVAL *and all.*) Ungrateful, insubordinate shower of Krauts! Of course all this seems very square to you, Miller, I daresay. What? All very middle class and stuffy, what?

BRINDSIEY. Oh no, sir. Not at all. Excellent sense. . . .

COLONEL. Yer think so?

BRINDSLEY. Bounders, absolutely bounders—all of them. Cads! Swine. Unspeakable! England is the last refuge of the scroundrel!

COLONEL. Are you pullin' my leg?

BRINDSLEY. Certainly not, sir! I wouldn't know where to start! (*Under the blanket,* MISS FURNIVAL *begins a muffled rendition of "Rock of Ages." All freeze. As she reaches the third phrase—"Let my tears flow evermore"—* CLEA *comes in above, from the bathroom, Stage Left, wearing the top half of* BRINDSLEY'S *pyjamas and nothing else. She carries her vodka bottle. She moves across the bedroom to the door.*) None of this evening is happening. Etc.

C.

Miss Furnival's speech "Prams! Prams!" is preceded by an alarmed noise under the blanket, a convulsive struggle, and a sudden throwing off of the blanket, as she gets to her feet.

D.

At the height of her speech, on "Keep off!" Schuppanzigh, drawn by the noise emerges through the curtains and shines his torch. Its light recalls her to herself.

Miss Furnival. Oh.

Harold. Come on, Ferny. I think it's time we went home.

Miss Furnival. Yes, you're quite right. I'm sorry. (*With an attempt at grandeur.*) I'm sorry I can't stay any longer, Mr. Miller, but your millionaire is unpardonably late. So typical of modern manners. Express my regrets, if you please.

Brindsley. Certainly.

(*Leaning on* Harold's *arm, she leaves the room. He shuts the door after her. There is an embarrassed pause.*)

Colonel. Confounded darkness.

Schuppanzigh. (*Softly.*) I am sorry. The fuse will be mended in a moment. Please, no one must come into the studio now, while the box is open. It is very dangerous, just for a few minutes. Excuse me. (*He disappears through the curtains. Stage brightens.*)

Colonel. (*Grimly.*) Never mind! The devil with yer fuse! I'm goin'. You can express my regrets too, Miller. Mine too, d'yer hear?

Carol. And mine, Brindsley. You can express mine! Etc.

E.

THE LAST SCENE, from the entry of Bamberger.

Bamberger. Hallo, please? . . . Mr. Miller? (*He walks slowly Downstage.*) Hallo, please?

Harold. Oh, it's the electrician!

Colonel. Well, what do *you* want? Have you mended that fuse yet?

Bamberger. Was ist denn diese Finsternis? . . . Brennt

hier kein licht? . . . (*"What all this darkness about? Is there no light?"*)

COLONEL. *What??*

BAMBERGER. Ist das ein schlechter Scherz? (*"Is this some kind of joke?"*)

COLONEL. Speak English, man, for God's sake. I don't want to hear yer filthy language!

(BAMBERGER *gropes his way Upstage towards the studio.*)

BAMBERGER. Das geht jetzt aber zu weit! . . . aber zu weit! (*"This is going too far!"*)

COLONEL. (*Shouting.*) Electrician, I'm talking to you!

SCHUPPANZIGH. (*Coming out through the curtains, carrying a large fuse.*) Hallo? Hallo, please?

BAMBERGER. (*In the same voice.*) Hallo? Hallo, please?

(BAMBERGER *disappears into the studio.*)

SCHUPPANZIGH. Ah no, that's not very funny. Just because I am a foreigner, to imitate my voice! You English can be the rudest people on earth!

COLONEL. Have you mended that fuse yet, sir?

HAROLD. Or are you going to keep us in the dark all night?

SCHUPPANZIGH. What does it matter? Do you think the light will improve your manners?

COLONEL. How dare you? Look you here, I'm giving you fair warning,—first thing in the morning I shall telephone your employers and see to it personally that you are fired. Do you hear? *Fired! (And indeed at this very moment* BAMBERGER *is "fired." Behind the curtain we see his silhouette in a shower of flashing sparks, transfixed by horror and electricity. He has evidently thrust his hand into the open main fuse box. Emitting little sharp howls, the millionaire rushes from the studio—a complete wreck: his hair stands straight on end, as if each strand were electrified; his face is blackened, and he is missing*

*half his beard. Without pausing for a moment, he hops galvanically out of the room and away into the night.*
[NOTE: *It is an easy matter for the actor playing* BAM-BERGER, *in the interval between his disappearance behind the curtain, and his electrocution, to change wigs and blacken his face. The assistance of an A.S.M would probably be necessary. It a wig is too difficult, half a top-hat could be used instead: and further dishevellment of dress, in the form of ripped-up collars, etc., will aid the picture.*])
Stop that whimpering, sir! You Germans are all alike! Bullys when you're winning! Cowards when you're licked! Now for the last time, get in there and mend that fuse!

SCHUPPANZIGH. (*Angrily.*) Don't worry. The fuse is mended. Much good may it do you! All of you! (*He goes back into the studio, brandishing the large fuse to insert into the box.*)

BRINDSLEY. Oh thank God! It's mended! Oh thank God! Thank God!

CLEA. (*Putting her hand over his mouth.*) Sssh!

HAROLD. I wouldn't thank him too soon, Brindsley, if I were you.

COLONEL. Nor would I, Brindsley, if *I* were you.

CAROL. Nor would I, Brinny Winny, if *I* were you.

SCHUPPANZIGH. (*Re-emerging without the fuse grandly.*) Then thank me! Though none of you deserve it, I will play God for this minute. Like Jehova in the Sacred Testament I bring you, miserable people, the most miraculous gift of the Creation—Light. (*During this last* HAROLD, *the* COLONEL *and* CAROL *slowly raise their weapons for the final attack.*) God said: "Let there be light. And there was, you wretches, suddenly!—astoundingly! instantaneously! inconceivably!—inexhaustibly! —inextinguishably and eternally: Light! (*He flicks on the light. Instead darkness. The Sousa march blazes away in the blackness.*)

*CURTAIN*

PROPERTY LIST

Statue with 2 detachable swordlike pieces
English telephone with 6-foot cord
2 cushions
18-foot wooden platform
Statue
Bureau
Bed with bedspread
Elevated platform

*On it:*
On onstage portion: CLEA's pajamas and makeup
Beat-up wooden chair
Beat-up wooden rocking chair
Stairs
Regency armchair
Crash box
Suitcase (HAROLD)
Small black table
Small blue-shaded lamp with 20-foot cord
Prop table with: 1 taper box matches, airline bag (for CLEA),
  SCHUPPANZIGH'S bag with flashlight
18-foot bench on blocks with: Statue of figure, ash tray, bucket
  of junk
4-legged bar table (3' x 4' x 2') with: 6 glasses, 1 ice bucket
  with fake ice, 1 bottle opener, 1 three-fourths full bottle of
  vodka, 1 full bottle of gin—top off, 1 full bottle of Scotch,
  1 bottle of lime juice, 3 bottles of Bitter Lemon, 1 syphon
  Seltzer
Regency chair
Throw rug
Statue
Beige pile rug with paint spots
Half-back Regency sofa
3 boxes lettered "A," "B," "C"
  Victrola
  Greek vase with fake daisies atop boxes
  Maraca on corner "C" box
  "C"—open faced with records and record rack inside

3-foot circular table with white brocade cover

*On it:*
Packing case (5' x 1½' x 1')
Disposable Buddha
Black Coalport vase

## PERSONAL PROPS

COLONEL MELKETT:
  2 cigarette lighters
  1 engagement ring

HAROLD:
  Matches

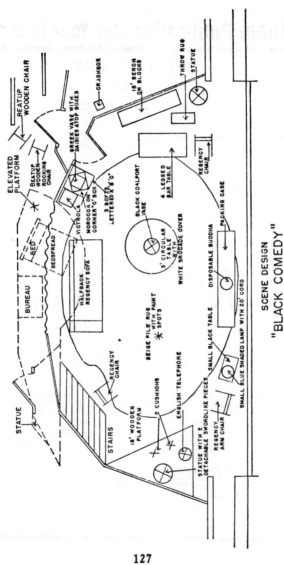

SCENE DESIGN
"BLACK COMEDY"

STATUE

STAIRS

18' WOODEN PLATFORM

REGENCY CHAIR

2 CUSHIONS

ENGLISH TELEPHONE

STATUE WITH 2 DETACHABLE SWORDLIKE PIECES

REGENCY ARM CHAIR

SMALL BLACK TABLE

SMALL BLUE SHADED LAMP WITH 20' CORD

BEIGE PILE RUG WITH PAINT SPOTS

HALFBACK REGENCY SOFA

BUREAU

BEDSPREAD

BED

ELEVATED PLATFORM

BEATUP WOODEN ROCKING CHAIR

BEATUP WOODEN CHAIR

VICTROLA

MOROCCO ON CORNER "C" BOX

3 BOXES LETTERED "A" "B" "C"

GREEK VASE WITH DAISIES ATOP BOXES

CRASHBOX

3' CIRCULAR TABLE WITH WHITE BROCADE COVER

BLACK COALPORT VASE

4 LEGGED BAR TABLE

18' BENCH ON BLOCKS

THROW RUG

STATUE

REGENCY CHAIR

PACKING CASE

DISPOSABLE BUDDHA